"It's a Pity Brenda Isn't Here,"

Maggie remarked. "Then you could be as romantic as you like."

"So that's it? You're jealous." Edan gave her a veiled look. "Well, Brenda is my affair."

"That's the point. Well, it's your life; you can keep it to yourself. And keep your hands off me."

"They aren't on you . . . not yet."

He emptied his glass and came closer. Suddenly his arms were around her, his lips covering her own with hungry, seeking kisses. Her bare arms circled his neck. He groaned. And they collapsed to the floor in a tangle of warm flesh.

HEATHER HILL
is a pseudonym for a bestselling author. This is her second contemporary romance for Silhouette Books.

Dear Reader:

I'd like to take this opportunity to thank you for all your support and encouragement of Silhouette Romances.

Many of you write in regularly, telling us what you like best about Silhouette, which authors are your favorites. This is a tremendous help to us as we strive to publish the best contemporary romances possible.

All the romances from Silhouette Books are for you, so enjoy this book and the many stories to come. I hope you'll continue to share your thoughts with us, and invite you to write to us at the address below:

Karen Solem
Editor-in-Chief
Silhouette Books
P.O. Box 769
New York, N.Y. 10019

HEATHER HILL
Lady Moon

Silhouette Romance

Published by Silhouette Books New York

America's Publisher of Contemporary Romance

Other Silhouette Books by Heather Hill

Green Paradise

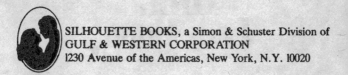

SILHOUETTE BOOKS, a Simon & Schuster Division of
GULF & WESTERN CORPORATION
1230 Avenue of the Americas, New York, N.Y. 10020

Distributed by Pocket Books

ISBN: 0-671-57171-0

First Silhouette Books printing August, 1982

10 9 8 7 6 5 4 3 2 1

Map by Tony Ferrara

America's Publisher of Contemporary Romance

Printed in the U.S.A.

Lady Moon

Chapter One

Maggie Jordan was late.

It was only an hour's drive from London to Deane Park but she had taken the wrong road at Bishop's Stortford. Now, turning in to the great stone gates, she felt a twinge of guilt. Lord Deane was the impatient sort. Her employer back in London, who knew him well, had warned her, so arriving late wasn't exactly the best way to begin an important assignment.

Better speed up, Maggie decided as she surveyed the narrow winding road that led through the Deane lands. The trail was empty as far as she could see, and she pushed down on the gas. The little red Morris convertible leaped ahead.

The morning was silvery-moist, not quite raining. After the city, it was a treat to breathe the air, and she half-closed her huge grey eyes to luxuriate in the fresh, wake-up sensation. She could feel the lift of thick, honey-colored hair as the wind caught it. Loyal as she was to her Connecticut home, Maggie was forced to admit that this bit of English countryside was as lovely as anything she had ever seen.

Deane Park, with its rolling hills, two thousand acres of trees and fields, and its miniature lake, was indeed a dreamworld. And she was about to enter.

There was an added touch of intrigue, too. The young Baron Deane was expecting the head of the firm, Peter Cross, a highly respected interior designer. He was *not* expecting a female assistant. But Peter had known Edan Deane at Oxford and he assured her that Deane might "stick at it right in the beginning," but that he would "come round." Furthermore, Lord Deane was bossy and a snob, but there was something about him that charmed. Not exactly a glowing recommendation. However, the job, decorating all the principal rooms in Deane Park, was such a plum that Maggie had swallowed her doubts. And here she was.

Well, I'm not about to be charmed, Maggie thought as the little car hugged the curves neatly, and I don't care how much of a snob he is as long as I get the job.

As she crested a rather steep hill, everything seemed to happen at once. First she caught a glimpse of the Georgian mansion on a distant rise, all pink brick and pale green roof. Then she saw the sign reading SLOW: Livestock Crossing. And suddenly a flock of sheep was meandering across the road right in front of her.

It would solve nothing to brake, for she would have hit at least one or two animals. She veered to the left and the Morris bumped over the rough grass, barely missing one of the sheep, and the engine died near an old stone bridge, with its wheels firmly in the stream.

Maggie groaned. Now what was she to do? Gunning the motor only made the wheels spin uselessly, as the car refused to budge. Perhaps the sensible thing to do was turn off the motor and think. At least she hadn't hit anything.

If she got out, she'd be standing in the stream, and

farewell to her mauve sandals, the ones that matched her cotton jacket dress so perfectly and had cost thirty pounds on the King's Road. She'd have to slip them off and wade ashore in her bare feet. As she bent over to unfasten the straps, a deep male voice tinged with annoyance startled her into looking up.

"Why are you trying to run down the sheep? Didn't you see the sign?"

A very large, very fierce-looking young man, mounted on an equally fierce black horse, was scowling at her from a nearby slope. The soiled and faded jeans, the casual shirt open to the midriff, indicated he must be one of Lord Deane's grounds keepers. Hired help or not, the man was strikingly handsome—somewhat shaggy black hair, well-muscled shoulders, strong brown hands at the reins, and brilliant black eyes that accused her of nameless crimes.

"Obviously I *didn't* see it, or I wouldn't be stuck here," she said, with more confidence than she felt.

"I suppose you expect me to pull you out."

"I'll manage without your help, thank you."

Again she bent to take off her shoes.

"Leave your shoes. I'll carry you out."

That made her straighten up in a hurry, and she gave him back as hard a look as she had received. Yet she felt at a disadvantage. Somehow it mattered that her hair was blown about and that under his harsh, dissecting gaze, the thin cotton of her dress—which she had thought so pretty only minutes ago—seemed totally inadequate.

With a bound he was off his horse and beside the car, his gum boots ankle-deep in water. Without trying to pull open the door, he scooped her up in his arms as if she were a doll.

"This is quite a bonus for a working man," he said, grinning down at her.

Seeing him so close, her face almost pressed against

his, she was aware of his full lips, the wicked little grin that revealed even white teeth. She tried to pull away from him, beating a fist against his chest, but it was hopeless—he just tightened his grip.

"Now none of that. Remember the old saying— 'Trespassers will be prosecuted!'"

"Put me ashore. Why are you just standing here in the middle of the stream?"

"Because I'm enjoying myself."

"Well, I'm not. And I'm not a trespasser. I have an appointment up at the house."

"Have you? Then I'd better help you on your way."

Though the tone was deep and musical, the voice held just a hint of ridicule, and Maggie could not help feeling he was making fun of her. She could hear the water rushing over the stones at his feet, as he stood perfectly still, defying her.

"Put me down immediately!"

She got no farther. With a sudden movement, he closed her lips with his in a hard, demanding kiss. A surge of anger flashed through her. He was nothing but a brute. A stranger. A servant. Just because he was strong and she was half his size, he thought he could do anything he liked!

Then without warning his lips turned soft. Gently, ever so gently he eased his mouth over hers and took it in. Made it his own. Made her flesh his flesh, moist and loving and complete. His arms drew her closer to his chest so that her breasts were crushed against him. His hand, caught in her skirt, seemed to burn through the thin material. Their bodies were close as they stood there like two entwined statues against the damp grey sky. Figures from another world. Maggie forgot for a moment where she was, the kiss was so loving, so pleasant. Forgot why she had come to this place.

But suddenly the memory of Peter's last words, just before she left London, broke into her dreamworld.

"This job is the most important one you've ever had, Maggie," he had said. "If you succeed at Deane Park, you can make a name for yourself in decorating circles. I'm giving you your big chance."

She pulled her mouth away from the stranger's mouth with a tremendous effort.

"What a—horrible thing to do!" she cried.

He grinned again and, with a sweeping gesture, set her down on the bank and turned away to deal with the car.

"If you ever want another kiss, just ask," he said. While she stormed and threatened to report him—"I'll tell Lord Deane how you behaved! He'll sack you!"—he jumped into the car and turned the key. She heard the motor turn over and knew that somehow, by what devil magic she could not imagine, he had started the car. As he backed it slowly out of the shallow water, although she was anxious to be on her way, she was even more furious that he had accomplished what she had failed to do.

"There we are, Miss," he said, making a silly gesture with his hand as if he were tugging at his forelock. "Do you want me to drive it over the grass to the bridge, or can you manage?"

"I can manage perfectly, thank you."

Thanking him came hard, for he was the worst example of male chauvinism she had ever encountered. She could not remember ever having felt such fury. At the same time, she wondered if she really should report him. Lord Deane would scarcely be impressed by her near-brush with his precious flock of sheep.

Bouncing the Morris over the ground toward the bridge, she could not resist looking back just once. He was motionless as a statue, mounted on the great black horse. She felt sure, even in the uncertain light, that he was smiling at her in that horrid sardonic way.

As she drove the final stretch—with extreme caution,

she silently promised Peter that she would do an excellent job, that she would placate Lord Deane for the change in plans and make him feel thrilled that a woman was decorating the house and not a man. She would ignore his snobbism, his rudeness. "I'll be so sugary, he'll think he's in heaven," she muttered to herself, just as she came to a stop before the house.

Maggie paused to consider the great house called Deane Park. It was every bit as beautiful as it had seemed in the distance, soft mist swirling and softening the outlines of the well-proportioned wings, the matching rose-brick bay windows. Even the two stone lions that crouched on either side of the path looked slightly hazy. The grass needed cutting. But she excused that when she recalled that Lord Deane had just come into the title and there was still only a small staff.

Deane Park had been empty for almost twenty years, except for the short period when it had been rented to a Finnish diplomat. For two decades the Deanes had lived on other estates throughout England. Such a waste, Maggie thought, when you considered its historic past.

Looking past the house, she could see acres of grassy slopes and magnificent groves of trees, the remains of formal gardens now overgrown with weeds, and the stream as it cut through the hills to the west. The lake shimmered among willows, and beside it she could see the folly—a small, round garden house with a dome and Grecian pillars. It was in these very gardens, many long years past, that Lord Byron had wooed Lady Caroline Lamb. Maggie was mad about Byron's poetry —and about Byron, for that matter. A wild, romantic, handsome adventurer who was always involved in some scandalous love affair. Byron's visit to Deane Park was one reason she had been ecstatic about its restoration. He and Lady Caroline had run hand-in-hand under these trees and probably made love in the folly. She almost expected the lovers to appear in this pastel landscape, emerging through the mist.

Before she stepped out of the car, the butler appeared to take her bags.

"I'm Bateman, Miss Jordan. Mr. Cross rang only a few minutes ago to explain. His Lordship was out so I took the call."

"I'm glad Mr. Cross got through. At least my arrival isn't a shock," she said. "I just have two bags, Bateman."

"This way, Miss. We have a room ready for you. But I hope you understand that the house is barely habitable. Mrs. Bateman has done what she could to make your room comfortable."

"Oh, I understand. That's why I'm here. To plan the decoration and refurnish the house."

The front hall was square and featured a staircase with two wings. It smelled a bit damp, the odor of a house that has not been lived in. That would all be changed soon, she thought happily. Peter had told her a little of the house, having once made a flying visit here with Edan Deane. Peter's own family had once been wealthy, and his connections in the social world were still excellent. He had turned his talents to decorating quite naturally, for as a child he had visited many great country houses and had learned to appreciate period furniture and good paintings.

As she climbed the stairs behind Bateman, she felt grateful that Peter had hired her as an assistant when she first came to London. Her prior experience had been limited to two restorations in Virginia, where she had worked as one of many assistants. But Peter said she had great talent and could go far in decorating and design, if she wanted to. He was just a little in love with her and once or twice had casually mentioned marriage, but she noticed that he took out several other women in London. And the Duchess of Elwyn, who wanted him to redecorate a number of important rooms in her main residence, adored Peter. It was because the Duchess had detained him at Elwyn House that he could not take on the restoration of Deane Park himself. Which was lucky for her, Maggie decided.

The butler was right. The bedroom he showed her into was barely livable, though it was spacious and light. The wallpaper was faded, the carpet shabby, and the furniture had been chosen at random. As Bateman set down her bags, she walked to one of the tall windows to look over the park. There was the folly. How pretty it looked from this angle.

"Is the folly still in good repair?" she asked.

"Oh, yes, Miss. The Finnish people who rented made it into a real picnic spot. They swam in the lake a good deal. They even built a sauna over there behind the cedar grove."

"A sauna? How wonderful!"

"Lord Deane uses it after a dip, I believe. Luncheon will be served at twelve, Miss Jordan, in the small dining room. His Lordship won't be back until dinnertime. He left that message for Mr. Cross. He also said—"

"But I had an appointment at eleven!"

"I'm sorry, Miss. That was his Lordship's message. He said to tell Mr. Cross to tour the house and grounds on his own so he could talk over the plans at dinner. I have the keys to the folly if you want them."

"Yes, thank you, Bateman. I'll do that."

With difficulty she concealed her annoyance. All that fuming about being on time, and now his *Lordship* wasn't even around! That fitted in with Peter's description of him. High-handed and bossy. Doing as he liked with no thought for others.

By noon Maggie had quickly toured the principal rooms: first, the drawing room, large and light, its main feature a white carved mantel. The white-and-gold wallpaper had been installed during the nineteenth century, and she made a note to inspect it for damage. Perhaps it could be retained and the restoration worked around it. Not a single piece of good furniture was left in this room, and she supposed they had been sold or stored somewhere. Next, the dining room, which contained one good piece—an Empire console supported by two sphinxes. But the dining table and matching chairs were mediocre. All the windows were beautifully proportioned, reaching from floor almost to ceiling.

Touches of white and gold would give some of the rooms a lift. But its delicate, dreamy quality was what made the house particularly attractive and that pastel flavor of a more romantic era ought to be kept, she decided.

Lunch was served in what had once been the card room. Mrs. Bateman, the housekeeper-cook, turned out to be a grey-haired, plump, pleasant woman.

As she put down a plate of cold salmon, she offered, "Now this is a nice little room, Miss. But the colors seem dull. It needs brightening a bit."

"Is it close to the kitchens?"

"Not really. But every room here is far from the kitchens, so it's as suitable as you'll find."

"It has possibilities," Maggie said. There was an arched niche in one corner that was empty now. But if it held a china collection it could be quite striking. She would have to enquire about Deane Park's possessions. Tonight at dinner, perhaps, when she confronted Lord Deane.

At seven o'clock Mrs. Bateman appeared at Maggie's bedroom door with a tray. A decanter of whisky, a syphon of soda, and a glass.

"Your before-dinner drink, Miss. His Lordship likes to dress for dinner."

"Thank you, Mrs. Bateman. Is there plenty of hot water?"

"In *your* bathroom, yes. The plumbing in some of the rooms isn't working very well. That's why I put you in here."

She had given her clothes to Mrs. Bateman to press when she first unpacked. Consequently, she had some choice of wardrobe. It was a cool evening and she decided on a grey silk with long sleeves and a rather high-cut neck. Best not to seem provocative. She would show Lord Deane that a woman could be businesslike and pleasant without trying to use her feminine wiles.

"His Lordship will be in the library when you come down. He usually takes a drink there at ten minutes to eight, before going in to dinner."

My, my, wasn't he a regimented type, Maggie thought. Issuing orders even when he wasn't there in person. Still, she was careful about her coiffure and makeup. Her hair was swept back with curls caught at the nape of the neck and a narrow pink-velvet bandeau to hold it smooth on top. Everything in good taste, with no flashy jewellery, only the wide ivory bracelet Peter had given her. When she viewed herself in the pier glass, ready to go down, she felt satisfied. Surely this somewhat demure outfit would please his Lordship.

When she entered the library at exactly ten to eight, it was lighted by only two lamps, and the shadows in the corners extended almost to the center of the room. Lord Deane was standing on the far side before a marble-topped commode bearing a drinks tray, his back to the door.

"I understand that my friend Peter has sent a surrogate," he said, without turning around. "Whisky?"

"Please."

Why did his voice sound familiar? That was strange. She knew perfectly well she had never met Lord Deane. In the dim light all she could see was the exquisite cut of his dinner jacket, and though he was bent slightly forward she was sure he was quite tall. And there was something about the shoulders . . .

"I must tell you, Miss Jordan, whoever you are, that I'm prepared to give you a drink and dinner, but tomorrow morning I must pack you off to London."

"Pack me off?" The arrogance of the man! As if she were some half-witted lackey from another age.

He poured. She could hear whisky splashing in the glass. He turned around. And then he grinned, a wicked grin that almost, but not quite, reached his dark eyes.

"The sheepkiller!" he said.

"I did not kill any of your sheep! How dare you pretend to me that you were a grounds keeper?"

"Now, Miss Jordan, I did *not* say I was a grounds keeper. You may have assumed that I was but—here, take this drink."

She accepted the glass, but she was still put out by his deception. "You didn't say that, but you knew what I thought."

He merely laughed. It was odd that she found his smile so attractive and yet so—well, just a touch devilish. She wondered if he treated the whole world like that—with a hint of ridicule.

"True, I did know what you thought. But I give you my word—the word of a gentleman, Miss Jordan, that I didn't dream you'd come here instead of Peter. I thought you'd come about some job with Mrs. Bateman. We're hiring extra help these days."

"Hiring extra help? You mean you thought I came here to apply for a housemaid's job? Really, Lord Deane, I find your attitude impossible. If that's how I appear to you, I'll be delighted to leave first thing in the morning, as early as possible. In fact, I may leave right now. Before dinner."

She was becoming more angry as she realized how he had regarded her out there in the park.

"Do have the drink first, at any rate," he said smoothly. "It's such a tiresome drive to London. And I suggest you wait until *after* dinner. That way, you'll have more energy."

"I don't want to dine with you."

"Because of what happened out there? Put it out of your mind. It was merely a whim. If I'd known you were Peter's assistant I wouldn't have kissed you. But he didn't let me know about his change of plans. I only found out a few minutes ago."

"You mean you're in the habit of kissing the hired help in that—that lascivious way?"

"I mean, you were attractive and I wanted to kiss you. I didn't think much about it."

"Oh, it only gets worse!" she cried, and then blushed as she remembered his mouth, his hands upon her, the heat of his body against her own.

"Then let's forget it, for the moment. Tell me about your job with Peter Cross. How long have you been with him? What's your background for this kind of work? You don't look old enough to have done much restoration."

"I worked on two houses in Virginia," she began defensively, "as an assistant. Then I came to London and met Peter through a designers' association. He offered me a job and I stayed."

"His offer had nothing to do with the fact that you're beautiful, I suppose? I know Peter. He has an eye for the ladies, always did."

"My credentials were what got me the position, not my looks," she said haughtily. "Peter needed a competent assistant and he liked my ideas."

"So you have a business relationship," Edan Deane said with another of his sardonic inflections. "Well, it's time to go in to dinner, Miss Jordan."

"Yes, it *is* a business relationship. Although we do go out to dinner sometimes—we carry our business meetings into the evening."

"Oh, all work and no play, Miss Jordan. I don't doubt it for a moment. Shall we go in? I like to eat promptly. Or are you still planning to leave before dinner, as you threatened?"

Across the dinner table, over the flickering of candles in silver sconces, she viewed Edan Deane and her will began to weaken. It was not because of *him,* she told herself. Definitely not. It was the job. She wanted desperately to restore this house. Already she had an affection for Deane Park. An affection based originally on the remembered tales about Byron and Lady Caroline, and supported by the innate beauty that she had strolled through only hours before.

During the afternoon she had inspected the lake, finding it clean and cool, fed by the clear stream that wandered over the Deane acres. The sauna was small, well-built, and obviously much used. She thought longingly of a swim and a sauna but decided that would be presumptuous until she had at least had a talk with Lord Deane and established that she was staying to do the job. As for the folly , it was delightful; in need of some small repairs, but in remarkably good shape, considering all things. The Finnish couple had bolstered up the window seat that circled the tiny room, and painted it cream. The walls were a pale leaf green. The light, coming as it did from every direction, was incredible, but not too bright, since it filtered through huge oak trees and chestnuts and laurels. She could imagine Byron and Caroline there, passionately flinging themselves into a mad affair with total abandon, defying convention and exhausting themselves in the pleasures of the flesh. . . .

"Now that you're here, you may as well give me your opinion," Edan Deane said, breaking her reverie as he poured from a bottle of Château Margaux. "I hope you like red wine."

"Yes, thank you, I do. . . . Why should I give my opinion if you have no intention of letting me do the restoration?"

"We have to talk about *something*, Miss Jordan."

"Very well, then. I love Deane Park. It's just as beautiful as I thought it would be. It's transparent—cool—rather like a watercolor. But I miss seeing any really important pieces. Are they stored in an attic somewhere? Just waiting for someone to discover them and bring them to life again?"

"My, you are a poet. I'm surprised that an American would have so much feeling for our history."

"Americans have feelings too, you know," she said icily.

"Oh, I know you have feelings. This morning when I kissed you, Miss Jordan, it seemed to me that you felt a good deal. I know it began only as a gallant gesture, but—"

"'What men call gallantry, and gods adultery,'" she said, crisply quoting Byron's *Don Juan.*

"So you know your Byron?"

"I've loved his poetry for years."

"Amazing. But then, as Byron himself said, 'Maidens like moths are ever caught by glare.'"

"'And Mammon wins his way where seraphs might despair,' to finish your quotation. That could apply to you, Lord Deane. Spoiled and rich and used to having your own way, regardless of others."

They glared at each other over the candles, fencing with words. Words written more than one hundred years earlier. The uncertain light pointed up the brooding power of Edan Dean's face, cast shadows against his tanned cheeks, outlined the full lips. And it polished the top of Maggie's blonde head and lighted the angry grey eyes, turning them luminous.

"This is ridiculous!" Edan exploded suddenly.

"It's your behavior that's made it ridiculous."

"Truce! Miss Jordan, I apologize for kissing you, for giving you assistance this morning, and for suggesting you were a barbarian who would not know poetry."

She ought to accept, she knew that. Lord Deane had taken advantage of her, true, and flatly refused to hire her for the restoration. But now he said he was sorry.

"I accept your apology."

"If you were older—or if you were a man—I'd give you the assignment just because you can quote Byron."

"And there you go again! You're the worst kind of chauvinist. Sex. Age. Just as Peter said. He warned me—"

"I gather Mr. Cross gave me a hearty recommendation."

She had made him angry again. Why did she have to talk on and on? Why couldn't she have shut up when she had the chance? Nevertheless, it was true. He had admitted that if she had been a man, she would have had the job without question.

"I'll leave in the morning," she said coldly.

"You may as well. Because you and I are not going to get along. You may have some notion of the historic importance of this house, but you're a child. What possible sense would there be to giving such an important commission to an inexperienced girl?"

"For you, none. You're prejudiced, and narrow, and Victorian. You belong in a world that's gone. You're an antique yourself—"

"I thought you liked old things, the old world, the history. You see, you don't know what you want!"

"I know I want to be respected. A woman can do any job as well as a man, and I intend to have a career and not knuckle under to some antiquated customs that are ridiculous, and—"

"You couldn't get the car out of the stream," he

pointed out. "I suggest you're mixed up. You don't really know what you're saying. Well, be a liberated woman if you like, and wait around for some man to pull you out of a river, or change a tire, or fix your engine. And then look at yourself. Foolish. Empty-headed."

"It won't make a bit of difference to you, so good night!"

She got up from the table, and threw down her napkin. Suddenly she wasn't hungry anyway. She had lost the job and insulted the man she had come to charm. She had let Peter down. And she wanted to cry. But she would not let Edan Deane see how very upset she was. She'd rather die. She fled the room.

Upstairs, she threw herself upon the bed, holding back her tears, and wished it were morning.

When she awoke, the room was flooded with sunshine, but her first thoughts were clouded by last night's argument and the fact that she had lost the job. Her watch showed six o'clock. She would have to pack her things and leave, hopefully without seeing the difficult Lord Deane. In all likelihood, she would never see Deane Park again, either. Even Peter's long friendship with Edan Deane wouldn't be enough to save the situation after last night's disaster.

She crossed the shabby carpet to the tall windows overlooking the little emerald lake. It certainly looked inviting, and the temptation to swim in it, to enjoy one final beautiful moment in the setting shared so long ago by Byron and Lady Caroline, was strong. If she went now, who would ever know? Certainly no one else would be up at this hour.

It hadn't occurred to her to pack a swimsuit, but since nobody was stirring, surely it would be safe to take a dip without one. She seized a large bath towel, put on jeans and a T-shirt, and made her way downstairs. Outside, the only sounds were the occasional calls of distant birds, the rustle of a thousand leaves, the whir of an insect hidden in the grass.

The lake lay clear as a mirror. From the wooden jetty she tested the temperature and found it rather cool. Near the bottom she could see a school of small, dark fish. The water looked about eight or nine feet deep off the dock, she thought.

She took off her shirt and jeans and slid into the water. It felt like cold silk against her skin. She swam for some time. Certainly the sun was higher when she emerged and grabbed the towel. Now, wet and shivering, she thought of the sauna. What a blessing that would be if she could use it!

The small wooden hut was unlocked. It smelled pleasantly of cedar. A bucket of coals was set ready to light and there was a full pail of water standing by. She set the coals on fire and waited, wrapped tightly in the towel. When they were hot enough, she threw on water and the coals hissed and exploded into steam.

Spreading her towel on the lower bunk, she lay down completely nude. A sweet sense of freedom, of utter relaxation flowed through her, making her feel just a bit wicked. For some reason, in the mounting heat, the memory of Edan's body against her own flashed into her mind. She closed her eyes and sighed. He *had* been quite gorgeous, now that she came to think of it.

But she forced herself to stop remembering. Edan had been rather nasty, and certainly he was a chauvinist. Imagine being unlucky enough to fall in love with a man like that! A man who quite obviously thought women were incompetent and shouldn't have careers! Horrible. He was a leftover from another age, that's what he was. Still, he did have a fascinating face. As for his body—she sank deliciously into a half-dream of half-formed thoughts. She was too preoccupied to hear the door open. Before she realized anyone had entered, before she opened her eyes, the door closed again with a tiny thud.

She blinked against the haze of steam. Edan's dark eyes were looking down on her, taking in every inch of her nakedness, as she lay stretched out on the bunk. She became conscious of her own body, of what those dark eyes could see—the taut, firm breasts peaked so uncontrollably, the flat stomach, the long, silken legs.

Edan Deane towered over her, smiling that terrible little smile, his teeth extraordinarily white in the gloom of the hut.

"Every morning a new bonus," he said, his eyes scooping up every detail. "And it gets better each day. Where will it all end?"

She scrambled to sit up, lifting her body off the towel in an effort to free it. For just a moment, she exposed even more than before, but at last she managed to drape the towel about herself and put her feet firmly on the floor.

"What are you doing here?"

It was a silly question. After all, it was Lord Deane's sauna, and he had every right to come in.

"I come here every morning. But I must say I've never had such fetching company before."

He moved closer, grinning maliciously. He wore a pair of bathing trunks and nothing else. They were wet, so obviously he had been swimming. Although she was oddly frightened and excited by his closeness, by his near-nakedness, she had to admit that he was magnificent. He was perfectly proportioned from the broad shoulders to the narrow waist and lean hips. His legs were long, and it seemed to her in that first moment of recognition that every muscle of his body was tensed and ready for action. She cringed behind the towel, and then rushed past him to the door. He reached out as if to stop her and touched her bare shoulder, but she spun away, turned the door handle, and was outside in the bright, fresh air. There her sense of panic fled. A cool breeze blew across her hot cheeks and calmed her racing senses.

But what if he followed? She snatched up her clothes from where she had left them in a heap on the grass and ran into one of the cedar groves to dress.

Edan Deane—drat the man!

Behind her, as she tugged on her jeans and pulled the T-shirt over her head, she heard his arrogant laugh and caught the sound of his insolent whistle—an old folk tune that seemed familiar. Then the words came to her: *Early one morning, just as the sun was rising, I heard a maid sing in the valley below. Oh, don't deceive me, oh, never leave me, how could you treat a poor maiden so?*

What a disgustingly arrogant man. She would leave, all right, as soon as she could throw her things into her suitcases. She wanted nothing more to do with the restoration of Deane Park or with the man who owned it.

But if that were the case, why was her heart pounding so?

Chapter Two

Maggie packed hurriedly, throwing her clothes in haphazardly. Then, lugging the two bags, she made her way to the garage without meeting a soul. The Morris sat where it had been parked by Bateman the day before. As she tossed her things in the back, she noticed a small puddle under the car. It had taken in water, yesterday, apparently. What a nuisance, she thought, turning the ignition key. Nothing happened. She tried again and again. Why hadn't she thought of this possibility and had the car checked!

The dismal whine went on, but the car failed to respond.

"Just where do you think *you're* going?" a deep male voice demanded.

And there he was, like some ferocious general about to do battle. Lord Deane, giving orders once again.

"I'm driving to London. Isn't that obvious?"

"Not if the car won't start. It must have shipped

water yesterday. Here, let me try. Get out. You aren't much of a driver."

"I'm an excellent driver." But she got out just the same, recalling yesterday's fiasco at the stream. This time, however, his magic failed to work. The engine refused to turn over. He climbed out, looking too large for the little Morris.

"I'll have Bateman send for a mechanic from the village."

"Thank you." She was always saying thank you, though she despised him. Really, it was impossible here and she wanted only to flee.

"Meanwhile, have you had breakfast?"

"I'm not hungry."

"You *are* rather a stupid girl. You need breakfast before you start out."

"So now I'm not only a woman, too young, inexperienced, and a bad driver, but stupid as well? I'll be glad to get back to London where I'm appreciated."

"Who will appreciate you? Peter's in Kent with the Duchess, I gather. Isn't that what you said?"

"Peter isn't the only man I know. I know men who treat me with some respect and who give me compliments—not like you—"

"You're very beautiful, Miss Jordan, and I know you must have a horde of admirers. And back in America, no doubt, you have armies of them. It reminds me of that poem by Houghton—not your darling Byron, I'm afraid, but apt just the same."

"Don't quote any more poetry, please. It doesn't help. You're still just as rude."

"But I insist. One more quote, dear lady, and I swear it'll be the last. 'Lady Moon, Lady Moon, where are you roving? Over the sea. Lady Moon, Lady Moon, whom are you loving? All that love me.'"

"Is that how you win all your women? Between the

poetry and the lechery, you're probably famous as a lover all over England."

"Look, I'm sorry about the sauna. But I couldn't help looking. You *are* lovely, you know. I take a swim every morning when the weather's decent, and how did I know there was a guest in the sauna?"

"You might have noticed my clothes outside."

"I might have. But I didn't. Come and have coffee, anyway. You Americans all like coffee, don't you? Mrs. Bateman's coffee is excellent."

She found, suddenly, that she was starving. The idea of hot coffee was appealing. It would be distasteful to face Lord Deane over the breakfast table, but the lure of food was too strong.

"I'll send Bateman for your bags. You'll need them. By the time we get the mechanic out here, and he either fixes your car or tows it away, it will mean staying another night."

"Surely there's a train?" she said, trying to catch up with his long stride, as she followed him back to the house.

"One every afternoon but it's a half-hour drive. I haven't time to take you today, I'm afraid. You see I really do act as grounds keeper. I haven't found all the hired help I need yet. So I make the rounds myself. That's why I was dressed like that yesterday."

"In that case, I'll wait for my car. I don't want to trouble you, Lord Deane."

"We're having a truce, remember? Could you call me Edan? Peter does, as I'm sure you know. If he and I can be friends, surely you and I can, too."

"I'll try."

"After all," he said, holding the door for her and bowing elaborately, "we are rather familiar with each other. I feel as if I know you . . . *intimately*, Miss Jordan . . . Maggie."

Sitting at the table in the sunny little dining room, she found that she could eat two helpings of scrambled eggs. Much as she would have liked to refuse, her appetite betrayed her. And the coffee was just as delicious as he had promised. She was on her second cup when she heard a woman's voice in the hall.

"Edan darling? Where are you?"

Watching him, Maggie could not be certain whether or not he was glad to see the woman who now glided into the room. She was tall and elegant in a grey riding habit. Her hair was dark and she had fair, English skin and light-blue eyes, which, as they fell upon Maggie, hardened perceptibly.

"Here we are, Brenda, come and join us."

Edan introduced her as Brenda Hawke.

"My next-door neighbor," he said. "She owns Chagford. Her land marches with mine, so we share a very long fence."

"And a very long history," Brenda added, with a meaningful inflection. "We've been friends for a long time. And who is this, Edan darling?"

"Miss Maggie Jordan. You remember Peter Cross, don't you? I went to Oxford with him. Well, I hired him to do some restoration on the house and he's sent his partner, Miss Jordan, instead," he said nonchalantly. "Peter's busy with the Duchess of Elwyn. Something world-shaking about her wallpaper, I believe."

"You mean you're really going to spend money on restoration?" Brenda demanded, taking a chair, though she seemed not to relish sitting at the table with a mere decorator.

He rang for Mrs. Bateman and ordered another cup brought for Brenda Hawke. Then he said lightly, "What's ridiculous about restoring Deane Park? It's a historic house and worth keeping up."

"I meant, darling, if you get married your wife will

probably want to redecorate. It's unlikely her taste would be the same as Miss Jordan's. So it would all be wasted."

"You think so? Well, my money's on Miss Jordan's taste. So I'm quite willing to take the risk."

"But you said—I thought I was—" Maggie began.

He held up his hand to stop her, fixing her with a piercing glance.

"Now, Miss Jordan, it's all settled. As I said to you only a few moments ago during our discussion, now that we're familiar with each other's little ways, we might as well go ahead with the plan. As soon as I saw your . . . qualifications, I knew instantly that Peter was right to send you out here. You're obviously the person to do the job."

He grinned at her provocatively.

"And what are Miss Jordan's qualifications?" Brenda demanded.

"She adores Byron, for one thing. Don't you, Miss Jordan?"

"All that gossip about Byron and Caroline Lamb is nonsense, if you ask me," Brenda said sharply. "If you counted every house in which Queen Elizabeth had a lover or Henry the Eighth slept, there wouldn't be enough beds in all of rural England. I doubt Byron ever set foot in this place."

"Would you like to see the original architect's drawings before you make another tour of the place?" Edan asked, ignoring Brenda. "If so, I'll put them in the library."

"That would be a good idea. There may be false walls, false ceilings. And then I want to find out where some of the important pieces of furniture have gotten to. I'll explore a bit."

"Good. I'll find them before I go out. Once you've breakfasted, perhaps you'd like to unpack?"

She expected him to add "again," but he didn't

comment further. She wondered if that was for Miss
Hawke's benefit. She was torn between accepting the
job, which she desperately needed, and telling him
coldly that she wanted nothing further to do with him.
If she stayed on, was he going to behave in this
outrageous fashion the whole time? But something in
Brenda Hawke's proprietary air, in her haughty manner, stirred Maggie's competitive instinct. Miss Hawke
fancied herself, there was no mistaking that. Well,
perhaps she didn't have Lord Deane under quite the
control she imagined.

She could always leave if he became too difficult,
Maggie decided. And she could call Peter and ask him
to pay a visit, too, to offer his opinion. So the case
wasn't lost yet. Yes, she would stay a day or two and see
how things went. That was the best plan. Edan Deane
was a horrible man, and clever, too, to have thrown this
at her in front of a stranger. Perhaps she ought to take
advantage of *him* for a change.

"I'm sure you can work things out with the hired help
at another time," Brenda cut in. "I rode over this
morning especially to talk to you about the condition of
the fences. Some of my cattle got through yesterday,
and it's dangerous because we never know what they
might eat. The fences obviously need mending and we
should come to some agreement about the cost. I
thought we could look over them together, Edan. It
would be perfect timing since my lawyer is coming
down from London to go over expenses with me this
afternoon."

"Certainly, Brenda, if you want to, but I don't know
what I can do about your cattle. I'm a bit short-handed.
We're still hiring help here, you know." His exaspera-
tion was evident. "Do you want to go right now?"

Brenda rose quickly, eager to get away.

"I'll see you at dinner, Miss Jordan," Edan said from
the doorway. "And I'll put those plans of the house on

the desk before I leave. No doubt you'll find them useful."

As they went out, Maggie heard Brenda say smoothly, "You know, Edan, it's a great pity our properties aren't all one. Then we'd have no problems about fences, darling, would we?"

Maggie didn't hear what Edan replied, but she told herself firmly that it didn't matter. Let Brenda Hawke have him, and welcome. Perhaps with *her* nature, she'd be a match for such a man, for she was as bossy as he.

Once she had unpacked for the second time, Maggie went downstairs to the library. She found the plans carefully laid out just as Edan had promised and sat down to study them before making a more detailed inspection of Deane Park.

There was the formal dining room to consider, with its tall window overlooking the grassy slopes of the park, and the First Drawing Room as well. Maggie liked the name of that room—it seemed to lend importance. She had already decided to preserve as much as possible of the décor except for the shabby carpet. The Deanes must have put their best carpets in storage somewhere. She made a note to ask Lord Deane about that. Otherwise, a large carpet would have to be purchased in London and that would run into a great deal of money.

The card room, used as the breakfast room, would take a bit of thinking about. At the moment she favored a yellow wallpaper with a springlike pattern. Fresh green leaves and birds perhaps. With big tubs of yellow chrysanthemums in the bay window. If she could find a china collection belonging to the family, she would fill in the niche that way.

Then there was the library: dreary now but of manageable size. Every large house should have at least one cosy room, a sort of lived-in place where the owners could settle comfortably for an evening. Had

Lord Deane considered that? Men were hopeless, though. They seemed to drift through their surroundings without paying much attention. Except for decorators like Peter Cross, of course.

Staring at the floor plans, the original architect's drawings, Maggie began to think in terms of the library. The classic white Adam mantel was the focal point, but the floor ought to be carpeted in something dark, to anchor the room. The furniture would liven it up—stuffed chairs and sofas covered in a black print brilliant with vermilion flowers and green leaves. And some vermilion cushions and chair seats to spot the color. A screen near the door would be useful to cut drafts.

One of her first considerations would be to find out just what Lord Deane actually owned in terms of furniture, paintings, and china. She ought to have enquired before he left this morning. Well, tonight at dinner would be soon enough. She would find out what the family had in storage. And the attic might yield discards that could be used, too. If a family's judgment was faulty, they may have put away things that were really treasures.

According to the plans, the storerooms extended across the third floor of the house. In this scheme, the servants' quarters were on the second floor in the back wing. It was in the attic, then, that she would find the discards of the past one hundred years—or even longer, disappearing as each generation decided to clear out furniture, books, and pictures they were tired of. Often families were not knowledgeable about antiques and it was common to find at least one handsome object, or even a valuable find, thrown casually into a corner under the eaves.

She had no difficulty getting into the attic. A flight of stairs led up there from the servants' wing. The first room was well lit from a row of small dormer windows.

It was dusty and crammed with furniture of every kind, as well as trunks, boxes, barrels, old suitcases, and numberless pictures. She began to pick through the paraphernalia, running her finger over the tops of tables and chests, pulling out a chair here and there, poking into trunks and giving a quick inspection to the stacks of pictures.

By noon, Maggie was covered with dust herself, but still enthusiastic. There was still so much to examine—she had barely begun, barely touched the jumble of possessions. Yet she had selected a pair of French armchairs which, with fresh upholstery, would make a nice addition to the library. Then, there was a painting —signed A. Nasmyth—that depicted Deane Park. Whether or not it was genuine was beside the point. It captured the romantic, pastel mood of the house and grounds and she could not imagine why it had been exiled up here. In any case, it ought to hang downstairs —perhaps in the front hall.

After washing up, she ate lunch by herself. There was no word from Lord Deane and she supposed a bit sourly that he was lunching with Brenda Hawke. Pushing away any thought of Edan and Brenda, refusing even to try to imagine what Chagford was like, she went to her room, changed into jeans, and then picked up a dust cloth from Mrs. Bateman. It was impossible to tell what kind of wood a piece was made of when it was under a layer of dirt.

This time she opened a window in the attic. Though the afternoon had turned dull, there was a fresh breeze that stirred up dust and loose papers but made the search more comfortable.

Time passed quickly. It was only when the light began to fail that she looked at her watch and realized it was after five. She ought to pack it in for the day, she decided, but couldn't resist pulling out just one more

piece—a bowfront chest that looked like satinwood
under the dust.

It was at this moment that she saw the door. Like the
famous one that confronted Alice, it was less than the
usual height, but it was beautifully made of walnut and
with a brass knob. By this time Maggie had worked her
way to the east end of the attic and had assumed that
this wall was the farthest corner. Judging by her
discovery, however, there must be yet another attic
room.

The door refused to budge. She turned the handle,
tugged, and banged without result. Perhaps, she
thought, there was an old-fashioned catch of some
kind. All sorts of romantic ideas rushed through her
mind. Was there a treasure hidden behind it? Was this
the hiding place of something precious to one of Edan's
ancestors?

She pressed around the handle with the tips of her
fingers, probing and pushing. And then, miracle of
miracles, she heard a click. This time, when she turned
the knob, the door swung open quite easily, and she
peered uncertainly into the dark shadows.

At first, it seemed to be just another small room, this
time with only one window. There were scattered
pieces of furniture, a box containing books, a harp. But
it was a small commode, the kind that might have been
used in a boudoir, that caught her attention. Though it
was covered with dust, the shape was interesting and
she thought the carving might be ormolu, a kind of
brass decoration often found on antique furniture. Her
dust cloth revealed a top of dark brown marble, curved
at the corners. There were two narrow doors on the
front and the whole was richly decorated with as fine an
example of ormolu as she had ever seen. When polished it would look like gold. The door fronts contained
the most fascinating feature, however—they were

made of bright blue and gold stone—materials very popular with French furniture makers. The blue was meant to imitate lapis lazuli.

Inside, she had hoped to find letters or perhaps a book with an inscription. When she saw only a small painting in a gilt frame, she felt a sharp disappointment. The work of an amateur, by the look of it, until she saw the signature and her heart stopped. *"Caro"*— that was what Lady Caroline Lamb had been called by her lover, Byron! And the painting depicted a man and a woman in front of the folly that still sat on the grass by the lake.

The man was darkly handsome with an aquiline nose and a fancy coat, and the woman was delicate and pale, a big straw hat resting on her lap. Maggie felt she couldn't breathe, she was so excited. Just wait until she took this to Lord Deane, just wait until she had a chance to show Brenda Hawke that this was indeed proof that Lady Caroline had visited Deane Park!

For she knew that Caroline Lamb had painted, in an amateurish way, and had written poetry, as well. The date of the painting could be ascertained in London and she would do that as soon as possible. Perhaps the little commode had been in the bedroom where Caroline slept. Maggie would certainly use the piece somewhere in the house. If only she could discover which room Caroline had slept in, it would be a perfect touch to place the commode there and hang the painting over it.

The breeze came up suddenly. Just as suddenly twilight fell and the shadows lengthened. As she peered at the little painting, the wind blew the door shut and the sound made her jump. The room was almost totally dark now, with only a faint glimmer from the single window. She felt instant panic.

All her life she had suffered from claustrophobia— fear of enclosed spaces, of being locked in. Now it was happening. She turned the knob, rattled the door, pounded the panels with her fists. Then, remembering, she began to press around the door handle, but this time she accomplished nothing. The door remained shut fast.

If only she had brought a flashlight! The darkness was crowding close and the air was stale and dusty. She must not panic, though. The window! She would open the window, that was it. And surely Mrs. Bateman would miss her, if she didn't turn up in her room to change for dinner?

It must be nearing six o'clock. What time would Edan come back from his day with Brenda Hawke? She ran to the window and found it nailed shut—she would have to break the glass. She seized a heavy glass inkwell and broke several tiny panes of glass, then pressing her face to it, she shouted into the fresh air. The wind came in now, cool and damp. That, at least, was a relief.

Careful, she must keep calm. Shout every few seconds or so and not wear herself out. Bateman might be outside, or one of the farm workers. Perhaps Edan would come riding up the road and hear her cries.

At times she shouted, at others she banged on the door. Finally she heard a voice that seemed close. Was somebody looking for her in the attic? She pounded on the door.

"Here! I'm in here!"

They might go away, they might not hear her. She banged and shouted, almost hysterical. For if they went away, whoever they were, convinced that she was not in the attic, it might be tomorrow before they came back this way again.

She felt the handle turn, then the door flew open and there he was, huge in the attic shadows, holding a flashlight.

Without thinking, she flung herself upon him, so glad

to see him that she forgot all her earlier feelings of anger and resentment. She was like a prisoner freed from jail, and when her body touched his in the friendly darkness, his strong arms automatically went around her and the metal flashlight fell to the floor. She could smell a mixture of cologne and the outdoors on his skin that was oddly exciting, could feel the roughness of his cheek on her own. His breath was hot against her ear and the warmth, the hardness of his body acted like a strong spell.

He pulled her tighter to him until the whole length of her body flowed into his, her breasts were pressed to his chest; she felt a thrill of pleasure as her thighs blended with his thighs. They clung together, forgetting everything, while he kissed her hair, her face, her neck, and she responded with no thought of tomorrow, or the day after, or the week after that. There was only now. Only this moment.

The breeze from the open windows billowed up little clouds of dust and ruffled her hair, stabbing her with its reality. What was she doing, throwing herself at this man? Letting him make love to her in this intimate way? She drew back, gasping.

"What's the matter? I thought you liked my kisses!"

It was the same slightly sarcastic voice. He was the same arrogant man she had met yesterday by the stream.

"Thank you. For saving me. I—I was afraid. How did you know where I was?"

"Bateman heard you shouting out the window," he said, stopping to pick up the flashlight. "Come downstairs and I'll pour you a stiff whisky. I think you need it."

She tried to back away, to gather up her dignity. She patted her hair into place and straightened her shirt, wondering if there were dust smudges on her face.

Then she scooped up the precious picture and stepped out of the ring of light that he beamed across the attic.

"I found an important picture," she began. "That's how I came to forget the door, I guess. I should have propped it open. But when I saw the commode—"

"You mean that this calamity is all because of a picture and a commode?" he asked in disbelief. "Isn't that like a woman!"

"What do you mean, *'like a woman'?* Because I feel something for history? Because I appreciate good furniture and colors and—and houses—are you trying to say that's a *fault?*"

"I meant that a man wouldn't forget to take precautions just because he saw a piece of antique furniture, or think a little painting was worth getting so excited about. That's all I meant. Come along, now, and we'll find that drink."

She followed him, fuming. Before coming to Deane Park, she had really thought that chauvinists like Edan Deane were extinct. But here he was. Proud and happy and very much alive. He ought to be stuffed and put in the British Museum, that's where he belonged. If Peter Cross had found the commode, or the picture, he would have been just as enthusiastic as she. But then Peter was infinitely more civilized than Lord Deane.

"I don't want your drink," she said, gritting her teeth.

"Now, now don't be touchy. I wasn't being critical. You're quite a woman, Miss Jordan. You kiss beautifully. With such enthusiasm, too! I value you. Don't misunderstand."

"Oh, I understand," she said grimly, still clutching the painting. "I understand exactly what you value."

"Here, let me see the thing that's caused all the trouble."

He took the picture from her and examined it.

"I can't say that it looks very valuable."

"Well, I only said it might be. It's only worth money if Lady Caroline painted it. That's what I intend to find out."

Maggie's intentions did not seem to impress him. He lighted the way down the attic stairs to the second-floor hallway and came to a halt before Maggie's bedroom door.

"If you don't want a drink right now, how about coming down a little before eight? We can meet in the library. Actually, I'm starved. Brenda keeps a rather poor table, you know. Lunch was scarcely sufficient to feed a sparrow. I'll have Mrs. Bateman send up your whisky tray immediately and you can have a leisurely drink with your bath."

He went off whistling. Maggie slammed her door to illustrate her anger. She wasn't to be appeased by his so-called hospitality. The sound of the banging door echoed like a knell in her mind. That was how she had gotten into this plight—by letting a door slam shut. Well, she would leave Deane Park first thing in the morning. House or no house, money or no money, Caroline Lamb or no Caroline Lamb, Lord Deane was intolerable. She set the precious picture carefully on the chest of drawers in her room. It continued to fascinate her. She knew that she would never rest until she discovered whether Lady Caroline had painted it with her own hand.

Chapter Three

She was deliberately slow about dressing for dinner. Just because Lord Deane wished her to appear in the library for a pre-dinner drink was no reason she should. He was far too accustomed to getting his own way. By careful planning, Maggie arrived downstairs at exactly eight and met Edan on his way to the dining room.

"You didn't come early enough for a sherry," he said. "I waited as long as I could. But it's time to go in, now."

"I didn't want a drink, thank you."

He glared at her. She knew he was cross. Everything and everybody was supposed to revolve around the wishes of Lord Deane. That much was abundantly clear.

They sat at the table, one at either end, and the air was frigid. Conversation was desultory.

"You found the plans?" he asked once.

"Yes, thank you, I did."

Over the rhubarb tart, Maggie made some attempt at conversation.

"I can't understand why you admire Lord Byron so much," she began. "After all, wasn't he a traitor to his class? I mean, supporting the Greek patriots?"

Edan Deane raised his eyebrows slightly—black, rather splendid eyebrows—and said, "That's exactly why I *do* admire him. Byron was a man of action. He wasn't afraid to stand up for his beliefs."

"But surely, as an aristocrat, you—"

"My dear Miss Jordan, you don't understand. Aristocrats were originally fighters. How do you think they got their titles in the first place? Usually for services rendered to the king. Most often in battles."

"And are *you* a fighter, Lord Deane?"

She knew she was provoking him, but his attitude made her want to argue. His arrogance, his superior manner definitely put her on the defensive.

"In my way."

He was being cool, trying hard not to lose his temper. She could see that. For just a moment she wondered if he imagined himself to be a modern version of Lord Byron.

"Well, if you're as notorious a lover as Lord Byron, you'll certainly go down in history. You seem to have roughly the same idea about women. Love them and leave them."

"You know absolutely nothing about me as a lover," Lord Deane said, rising and giving her a furious look. "Do you wish to join me for coffee in the library, Miss Jordan?"

"Oh, I think I know a little," she began. "Our first meeting, and up there in the attic, too. Surely that qualifies me to make some statement?"

She knew she was behaving in a way that would irritate him. Yet, she reasoned, he had certainly taken advantage of her, putting his arms around her that way, and kissing her. By his behavior, he had asked for criticism.

"Nothing that's happened so far qualifies you to comment on me in that way. Your reactions have been hysterical. Do you wish to join me for coffee?"

She wanted to say that nothing in the world would make her share an after-dinner coffee with him. She only wished to get away from him, because every time they were together, there was an unpleasant scene of some kind.

"Thank you, but I'm tired. I'll just go up to bed."

As she ascended the stairs, she could feel those dark, brilliant eyes watching her every move. At the top, she could not seem to resist looking back. Their eyes met.

"I have never loved any woman," Lord Deane said. "And I have never left one. Good night, Miss Jordan."

Maggie did not sleep well that night. On the one hand, she wanted to leave Deane Park to preserve her dignity. On the other, she had already come to love the place and the idea of doing a bit of detective work to establish who painted the little picture gave her a thrill of anticipation. It was just such details that made restoration worthwhile. As a consequence, she swung from sleep to waking, and from a decision to leave to a determination to stay, all through the hours of the night.

If she had hoped to avoid Edan Deane at breakfast, she was disappointed. When she entered the card room, there he was, large as life, drinking his coffee and reading a day-old copy of the *Times*. He offered her a broad smile as if nothing had happened between them.

Just like a man, she thought—really dense. He tells me I'm inadequate and that I locked myself in the attic because I'm a woman, then he tries to make love to me and thinks I'll be delighted.

"How are we this morning?" he asked, putting down his paper and rising politely until she was seated.

"*We* are fine," she said crossly. He was even more impossible than she had remembered during the night.

"What are your plans for this morning? Going up to the attic again? If so, you'd better leave a trail of bread crumbs."

The smile was as dazzling as ever, the eyes as unfathomable, the shoulders as broad. It wasn't fair. What a great pity, she told herself, that she had begun to actually hate him. What a shame he was despicable and arrogant, for otherwise he would have been quite attractive.

"I won't be going to the attic, or anywhere else. I won't be in charge of restoring Deane Park. I've had time to think about things, Lord Deane, and I realize we can't possibly get along. We see everything differently. I made a real find yesterday and you think it's all a joke. A man like you shouldn't be the owner of a historic property like this. You haven't the taste. I can't think how it happened."

For just a moment, she thought his anger might flash out at her. Perhaps she had gone too far. The hand resting on the newspaper clenched into a fist; the wild temper seemed on the verge of exploding.

"Would you like to see my family tree? That will explain to you how it happened. You see, one of my ancestors was with the Barons at the signing of the Magna Carta—then, after that, there was his son, who married Lady Cardith, who in turn—"

"Since I'm leaving, there's no use telling me," she said, spreading a white linen napkin precisely on her lap, as Mrs. Bateman came in with fresh coffee.

"So many of my friends are Americans," Edan said by way of explanation, "that I've trained my staff to serve coffee first thing. But would you like fresh fruit, or juice?"

She spoke directly to Mrs. Bateman, ignoring him. "Grapefruit, please."

"Yes, Miss. I have it ready."

"By the way, Miss Jordan, do you ride?" said Edan.

She was thrown off stride by the sudden change of subject, but she replied politely.

"Not very well, but I do ride if the horse is manageable."

"Good. Then you can come with us this morning. I'm taking the new groom on a tour of the property."

"I told you, I'm leaving."

"Your car isn't ready. I've already telephoned the village. Perhaps later this afternoon."

"I see."

"So there's nothing for you to do. You don't want to waste your time on the house, making notes, thinking hard, if you aren't going to do the job. Why not come out with us? It's a beautiful day."

She had taken a few riding lessons at the time she worked on one of the historic houses of Virginia, and if the horse was gentle, she could ride well enough.

"Do you have a horse that's easy to handle? I'm not a skilled rider like Miss Hawke, I'm afraid."

"I'm sure we can find one. Miss Hawke is a magnificent rider, but of course she's been around horses all her life. Her father was master of the local hunt for a long time."

"You two *do* have a lot in common. Your houses, your horses, your fences . . ."

"Do I detect a malicious note?"

"Hardly, Lord Deane. Why would I be interested? I prefer living in London and I love my career. I wouldn't live out here in the country for anything in the world."

He sighed and pushed a bit of kipper around on his plate, like a spoiled child who threatens not to eat in order to get his own way. Even in such a mild argument as this, Lord Deane apparently hated to be crossed.

"Well, each to his own. I love the country. When I was a child we seldom lived in this house, because my mother preferred our place in Kent. But I always had a special feeling for Deane Park. I decided long ago that when I came into the title, I'd make it my main residence. Something to do with Lord Byron, perhaps. I wrote a thesis on him in college. About the way in which his poetry reflects events in his personal life."

"*Did* you?" She couldn't help being pleasantly surprised. "You didn't say that last night."

"I didn't have a chance."

"You mean you admired the romantic side of him as well as his radical politics? Judging from last night, I thought . . ."

"You know, Miss Jordan, you're rather hasty in your judgments. Anyway, it takes courage to write about one's deeper feelings. As much courage as it takes to fight a battle. Would you like to read my thesis sometime?"

"I'd love to read it."

She had forgotten, momentarily, that she planned to leave Deane Park.

"I'll find the paper for you after lunch. But this morning I'd like you to ride with me. I have to look in on a fellow I hired to look after the horses and grounds. These days everyone does two jobs, I'm afraid. Help is so scarce and so expensive."

She saw a cloud of worry pass over his face. This was the serious side of Lord Deane, the brows drawn together in a slight frown, the mouth no longer smiling or sarcastic, but set in a determined line. For the first time since her arrival, she realized just how much responsibility he had in running Deane Park, and how many problems such a huge property could entail.

"How many horses do you have in the stables, then?"

"Four mounts and half a dozen work horses. I've just

taken on this young fellow and I hope he likes it here. He's a gypsy."

"A gypsy?"

"Well, he came from a gypsy band. But he says he wants to fit into a more secure life. The men are marvellous with horses. Most of them are trained as farriers and veterinarians. They can turn a hand to anything connected with horses."

"He sounds wonderful."

She had never met an English gypsy, although she'd often heard about them. Since it was to be her last day at Deane Park, she might as well go off with him and try to enjoy it.

She put on jeans and a shirt and met Edan Deane at the stables. His big black stallion was already saddled and ready, and she caught sight of the new groom as he vanished inside the stable to bring out a mount for her.

At a guess, he wasn't much older than she was. She suspected that he was strong, despite his thin and wiry build. His complexion was swarthy, burned by long hours in the sun, his dark hair curled tightly, and his eyes were such a dark brown that they were almost black.

As the groom brought out a small filly, Edan Deane made the introductions, "This is Quinn, our new groom. Quinn, I'd like you to meet Miss Jordan. She'll be working here, too, for awhile."

Maggie glared at him for that. He knew perfectly well she was leaving. Why did he say such things?

Quinn helped her to mount, checked the girth solicitously, and patted the animal on the nose.

"Don't you worry, Miss. She's gentle as one of them lambs out there."

"Thank you, Quinn. I'm not very experienced."

"Stay by me," Edan said, "and you'll have no problems."

Quinn, mounting his horse with the grace of an

acrobat, waited for them to lead. But his own riding skill and natural impatience soon brought him alongside.

"You're doing very well, Miss Jordan. Anytime you want a few pointers, you come out and I'll be glad to help. Anytime I'm not busy, of course."

"That's kind."

I wish I *were* staying on, she thought a bit irrelevantly, so I could learn to ride really well. Quinn, whenever she looked in his direction, seemed friendly, but he had a brooding look. She wondered if he missed the old life, and if he would really settle into the routine of Deane Park.

Certainly Quinn was serious about his work. He listened to everything Edan Deane said and took in all the instructions, all the bits of information about the huge property that might be useful in his job.

As they made the rounds of the tenant farms, Maggie herself came to realize more and more how much work Edan must supervise, how many decisions he must make.

"You wait here," he said, as he dismounted at one cottage. "I usually speak to Farraday myself. He's getting hard of hearing. He was head gardener for my father and we pensioned him off. He lives in the cottage rent-free, of course, and grows a small vegetable garden. But I often wonder if he gets enough to eat."

They waited while he visited the old gardener. The cottage was small and neat, with a thatched roof and a well-clipped hedge. When Edan came out again, he was shaking his head.

"He's all excited about a new litter of pups in there. But I'll have Mrs. Bateman send him over a food hamper, just the same. I think he lives on sandwiches when nobody cooks for him."

Maggie was touched by Lord Deane's concern for the old man. However, she told herself sternly, his attitude toward retired servants did not alter his appalling view of women. She did not say much on the way back to the stables, but when she dismounted, Quinn reminded her of his offer to give her lessons. She felt a bit sad to think that she wouldn't be here to take advantage of it.

It was almost noon and the sun was high. Maggie felt desperately in need of a shower and change before lunch.

"Well, what do you think of Quinn?" Edan asked as they entered the house. "Do you think he likes it here?"

"Oh, yes, he loves it here! He seems to have some worry on his mind, though. But he's certainly eager to learn."

As they crossed the hall together, Bateman appeared.

"Miss Jordan, your car is back. The mechanic reports it's fixed and running nicely."

"Thank you, Bateman. That's fine."

She almost added, "I'll be leaving this afternoon," but stopped herself. The ride had mellowed her feelings for Edan Deane. She had seen him in a new light. And for the first time, she was flooded with the sensation of wanting to stay on at Deane Park, of becoming a part of life here. This world was not dull as she had imagined, but filled with small events: Lord Deane and the old gardener, the new groom and his rather exotic background, and the constant concern with restoring the splendid house and park. There was just as much going on in the country as there was in her London existence, but it was of a different quality. Yet there was a feeling of importance, of—she searched for a word—of *majesty*, about life on an estate.

"You really think he'll settle down? That he'll stay on? I've watched him with the horses and he's a wonder," Edan persisted.

"I'm sure of it. Quinn will probably turn out to be a very valuable employee."

"Good. That's what I think, too. I'm glad we agree on *something*, Maggie Jordan."

As she turned in to her own room, Maggie found herself in the same frame of mind. The mood continued throughout lunch. Neither of them mentioned her plan to leave that afternoon. It was as if they were both deliberately avoiding the very subject that was uppermost in their minds. Halfway through the meat course, Mrs. Bateman came in to say that Maggie was wanted on the telephone. It was London.

"London? Oh!" Maggie crumpled her napkin and placed it on the table, then followed Mrs. Bateman out into the front hall. Why was Peter calling her now?

"Hello, Maggie," Peter said cheerily. "How are you doing with the fierce Lord Deane? Have you tamed him yet?"

"Peter!" She was glad to hear his familiar voice. "Why aren't you with the Duchess?"

"I got time off for bad behavior, my sweet. I told the Duchess I had to be in London for a couple of days to look for rare wallpaper. She's entertaining, but a bit wearing. I needed a break. So I thought I'd sneak over to Deane Park to consult with you and Edan about the job. Perhaps stay the night, if Edan begs me."

"You'd better talk to Lord Deane," she said cautiosly.

She was reluctant to tell Peter she had decided to resign even before she started. He'd be so disappointed. And she'd have to listen to a lecture about how important it was to her career to make a success of the house.

After a brief conversation with Edan, Peter told her they had agreed that he ought to come out for dinner and the night. She hung up, wondering why she had consented, why she had been too cowardly to tell Peter the truth.

"I'll call Brenda and see if she'll join us for a swim and dinner," Edan said over coffee. "We'll make a lovely foursome. You can have another sauna."

"You know perfectly well I have no swimsuit with me."

"That didn't stop you yesterday, as I recall," he said, looking wistful. "I distinctly remember—"

"Let's not hear about what you distinctly remember," she said sharply. "Just where do you think Peter is going to sleep? Who is going to make all these arrangements for dinner and a house guest?"

"You are."

"I am? Why should I?"

"Because I have to spend the afternoon on the Easter Wood Lot, choosing trees to be cut and sold for lumber. A very exacting job. Do you know anything about trees?"

"Certainly not. But I don't see why—"

"Then it's clear that I'll have to choose the trees to be sold while you find a bedroom for your boss. You do know something about cooking, surely?"

"I consider myself to be a good cook," she said defensively. "But handling a dinner party in another person's house is—"

"It's all settled. See you at five. Peter said he'd be here about then."

He took off, leaving her to consult with Mrs. Bateman about a guest room and a menu. Although she was annoyed, she decided she must go ahead, otherwise Peter would be embarrassed. She couldn't make a scene. She would explain quietly to Peter that she couldn't stay here at Deane Park. Perhaps after dinner, perhaps the next morning. Yes, that was it. She would appear at breakfast, and tell him she was going back to

London. That way, everyone could at least enjoy a
pleasant evening. If there was such a thing as a pleasant
evening in Edan Deane's company. And that snob,
Brenda Hawke.

Between them, she and Mrs. Bateman chose one of
the bedrooms that could be made habitable quickly.
The room had no adjoining bathroom, but there was
one close by that worked sufficiently well. It was only
for a night, she reasoned. Peter would have to make do,
since it was his idea to come out to Deane Park.

Peter drove up at about five o'clock. She was already
in the library waiting when Bateman announced him.

As he came quickly through the door, Maggie felt a
pleasant sense of relief and comfort. There he was, tall,
blond, blue-eyed, and good-natured. Smiling, hugging
her, kissing her on both cheeks.

"What a lovely reception committee," he said. "You
seem to have fitted right in. I knew you'd love this
house, with your fancies about Byron. How are you
getting on with Edan?"

"All right, I guess," she said evasively.

"Where is he?"

"Out choosing trees to be cut for lumber. On the
Easter Wood Lot, I think he said. Could I mix you a
drink? I see the tray is here."

"A whisky and soda. My, we are the little domestic,
aren't we? 'The Lord and Master is out on the wood
lot. Let me make you a whiskey and soda, my dear.'"

His imitation was good-natured. She saw at once that
she had given a totally wrong impression: that she
seemed to be settled in comfortably, when in truth she
was about to flee.

"It isn't like that at all," she protested, handing him
his drink. "I happen to know how you like your drink
made, that's all, and Edan isn't here."

"You like the house?" Peter asked anxiously, settling
into one of the armchairs and studying her. "It has

great charm, don't you think? Tell me your ideas so far."

"Yes, it's a beautiful house. You were right. I adore it."

She was tempted to say, "But I can't stay." Instead, she added, "I found a painting. I think Lady Caroline painted it—it's amateurish but pretty. I thought I'd take it to London and see if I can authenticate it somehow. At least, that's what I . . ." She stopped herself from revealing the truth about her situation at Deane Park.

"Of course, you must take it in," Peter said enthusiastically. "You'll have to go in for materials and carpets anyway, once you've made your decisions about color schemes. Go to the Academy at Burlington House. You know Everly Jones, there, don't you? He'll steer you right."

He was obviously delighted at what he thought was her great success at Deane Park. How disappointed he would be when he found out she had no intention of restoring the place. They were interrupted by an apologetic Mrs. Bateman.

"Could I speak to you about the menu, Miss Jordan?"

Maggie saw the worried frown on the housekeeper's face. Something had gone wrong. Two hours before dinner and they were in trouble. She excused herself and followed Mrs. Bateman.

"What's wrong, Mrs. Bateman?"

"The trout hasn't arrived. It was to be delivered and now I have no fish course. His Lordship particularly asked that we serve every course tonight. He's always fussy when *she's* coming. I mean, Miss Hawke."

Yes, I imagine he is, Maggie thought angrily. He wants to impress her. So why should I fume over dinner for Miss Hawke? Still, Edan was depending upon her.

"Then scratch the idea of trout. Have you any other fish?"

"Flounder. It's frozen, but it doesn't take long to defrost it. The filets are thin."

"Good. Then we'll use that. I have a marvellous recipe for stuffed flounder. I can make it ahead of time. Just so long as you have mushrooms and crabmeat."

"Tinned crab, Miss. Is that all right?"

"That's perfect. I'll need some fresh parsley from the garden and a dry white wine. I'll come down to the kitchens before I dress, Mrs. Bateman, and make it up for you. All you have to do is put the fish in the oven about half an hour before serving time."

Mrs. Bateman looked greatly relieved.

"Thank you, Miss Jordan. That does make me feel better. His Lordship hasn't come back yet and I can't ask his opinion. He counts on his dinner parties being just right."

"Everything will be just right," Maggie said grimly. "We must keep Miss Hawke happy."

When she returned to the library, Peter was ready for another whisky. He continued to tease her about her new role. Although he was laughing, she had a feeling he was annoyed.

"I never expected to see you play the chatelaine," he said. "It must be the country air."

"You aren't jealous?" she teased.

"Good heavens, no! I'm glad you're getting on so well with Edan. He's rather a difficult person in some ways."

Edan appeared shortly thereafter and then Brenda Hawke. It was such a warm evening that they decided to have before-dinner drinks down at the lake. Brenda then announced that she would swim. Edan said he thought that an excellent idea, since they were all dressed casually. So Bateman brought a portable bar down to the edge of the water.

Brenda changed in the sauna hut. When she came out wearing a sleek one piece black suit, provocatively hitched up at the thighs, Maggie felt a stab of envy. She saw the look of appreciation the men wore. They made jokes about Maggie swimming without a suit, but she refused to bite, opting to sit primly in her white polished cotton with its string straps. The dress was revealing without being too obvious, and for that reason she had always favored it. But seeing Brenda in the wet black suit, she felt spinsterish.

Dinner, however, went smoothly. Edan and Peter reminisced about their days at Oxford, Brenda pretended to listen attentively, the fish course was pronounced delicious, and eventually talk turned to Deane Park and the restoration.

"Did Maggie tell you about the painting she found? And how she locked herself in the attic?" Edan asked.

"Don't tell me you've had adventures so soon!" Peter said. "She mentioned a picture, but not the rescue."

"I was her personal white knight. Not on a charger, of course, and armed with a flashlight, not a sword. But still we managed to turn it into a . . . memorable moment, didn't we, Maggie?"

"It was nothing." Maggie sniffed. "Not worth mentioning."

"Ah, but the picture could be important. It might prove that Lady Caroline really stayed in this house."

"You're surely not going on and on with that old fairy story?" Brenda said, barely concealing her boredom.

"We'll let you know about that once the painting is authenticated. After Miss Jordan takes the picture to London, isn't that right, Miss Jordan?" Edan had reverted to formal address in putting her on the spot. He was actually daring her to announce that she was quitting, that she wasn't going on with the assignment.

"I intend to try," Maggie said, looking directly at Brenda. "Because if the painting was done by Lady Caroline, she must have visited Deane Park. Otherwise, how could she have known the details of the folly?"

By eleven o'clock, Brenda was in her car and off to Chagford. The night had not grown cooler. Even the patio was stifling, and Edan announced that he always retired early so he could get up first thing in the morning to supervise the work. Peter was restless but admitted the routine at Deane Park was a change from attending the Duchess, who was such a nighthawk she felt everyone ought to stay up and amuse her until two or three every morning. Finally Edan, Peter, and Maggie bade each other good night.

It was one of those utterly still nights when not a leaf moved, not a bird swooped through the scattered treetops. Maggie opened her bedroom windows but it brought no relief. She propped open the door, hoping to catch a breeze. There was none. After tossing about for an hour, she was still wide awake. Anything would be better than this, she reasoned. Surely out at the lake it would be cooler?

She pulled on a silk housecoat and padded out into the hall. A shaft of moonlight revealed every detail of the staircase and she had no need of a flashlight. She tiptoed downstairs, being careful not to disturb anyone. After all, Peter and Edan might be having more success finding sleep than she. On the lower level every door was open in an attempt to trap a waft of cooler air.

It was the "rent room" that attracted her, set at the back of the house, its French windows opening into the garden. A broad patch of moonlight splashed across the carpet. Actually, the rent room was a small office in which former owners of Deane Park had collected rent from the tenants each month. Though it was no longer

in use, the old table was still there, with its special
drawers for holding papers and money.

The room took on a luminous glow. She could almost
see the tenants in their old-fashioned clothes, lined up
to pay the rent, and the master sitting sternly behind
the table like a presiding judge. Caught in this fancy,
Maggie began to imagine uses for the present day. The
room would be cosy in winter—there was a generous
fireplace—and with planning it could be refreshing in
summer, too. A new garden might be planted outside
the windows, adding a whole new dimension.

She leaned against the frame of the French windows,
so deep in her thoughts that she failed to hear approaching footsteps. When she turned at the sound of
someone in the doorway, she gasped, thinking it was a
stranger.

"Who is it?"

"Maggie—it's only me, Edan."

"Oh, thank goodness! You frightened me."

"I'm sorry. I heard someone wandering about and
thought something was wrong."

"Nothing's wrong. I couldn't sleep."

"You look so lovely there. Do you know that line
from Sir Walter Scott—'If thou would'st view fair
Melrose aright, Go visit it by the pale moonlight'? . . .
I never thought of applying it to Deane Park before."

"Now, really, Lord Deane, don't start all that
again."

"Why the formality? I thought we were on a first-
name basis at dinner."

"Were we?"

It seemed natural that he come toward her. Natural
that she remain perfectly still. He towered over her and
she realized once again how broad-shouldered he was.
At almost the same moment, she became aware of her
flimsy nightwear and her own vulnerability. Yet she did
not run away.

"You know, Maggie Jordan," he said softly, "You're the most beautiful woman I've ever seen. I'll always remember you standing just there, under the moon, as if you belong here, as if you've always been a part of this house."

His voice held none of the old brashness, none of the playful, slightly disdainful tone she had come to expect. For this little time, at least, Edan Deane seemed very warm, a man in need of love. Perhaps even something more—a dream to cherish. A dream that would last forever.

When he put a hand on her shoulder to turn her toward him, Maggie did not resist. His touch was possessive but there was no force. Rather, it was light and caring. The same tingle of excitement ran through her as that first time when he kissed her by the stream. Yet it held a new quality. A secure, wonderful feeling.

But this is madness! she told herself. Even when his dark eyes looked deep into hers, questioning, willing, seeking, she knew she must not let him dominate her like this. She knew what kind of man he was. Hadn't he demonstrated it over and over? She must retreat. She must not allow herself to be won so easily by yet another of Lord Deane's little tricks.

He gathered her slowly into his arms, holding her tenderly. The warmth of his body flowed into hers. An intimate, magic mood wrapped itself around them, more dangerous than any quick passion.

As they clung together, completely absorbed, a bright light shone on them from the doorway.

"What's going on? Everything all right here?"

Maggie recognized the voice as Peter's. There he was, holding a flashlight and peering at them.

"I'm sorry. I thought someone had broken into the house."

"So did I, so I guess it's in the air," Edan said

quickly. "But it was only Maggie. She couldn't sleep. I found her here working overtime. She never knows when to stop, this girl."

Peter, obviously embarrassed, laughed thinly.

"Well, then, I'll just go back to bed," he said lamely.

"That's what we're all going to do," Edan said firmly. "Come along, Maggie. Perhaps you can sleep now."

They straggled back upstairs, all unsure of exactly what to say. Maggie wished she had more clothes on. She didn't like being so exposed before the two of them. It seemed all wrong.

Even after she had settled down again in her own room, Maggie found it hard to fall asleep. For a brief flash, she had seen a different side of Edan Deane. Or had she imagined it?

At the breakfast table, Peter was cool.

"Look, I must get back to London right away. The Duchess is expecting me for dinner tonight and it's another longish drive from London to Elwyn House. I have to pick up some samples this afternoon, as well. To show I've been working." He gave a short, artificial laugh.

"I'll be in London myself in a day or two," Maggie offered, avoiding Peter's gaze. "I'm not quite ready to shop around yet, of course, but I have some ideas. I thought I'd take the picture in with me, and the commode as well. That's where I found the painting so it might be important. I'd like to have its date fixed."

She knew she was speaking too quickly but she felt nervous. She smiled tentatively at Peter.

"Very well, if that's your plan. I'll talk to you then. Call me from the office and let me know how you get on. Although I must say you seem to be getting on rather well."

Later as they watched him drive off, Edan said apologetically, "I put you in rather a bad position last night. It's my fault. I'm sorry. After all, Peter's your employer and he's fond of you. If I were in his position, I'd probably shoot any man I found kissing you."

"There is no 'position,' as you put it. Peter has been good to me. We're friends, that's all."

"Good. I notice you didn't tell him you're giving up the job."

"I meant to tell him this morning. But after last night, I'm not so sure, although—" She trailed off uncertainly.

"If what happened last night makes you stay on here, I'm glad. So I'll stop apologizing."

"If I stay on, it's because I consider it good business. Nothing more," she said flatly.

"Let's say no more about it then. And I hope you'll take up Quinn's offer to give you riding lessons. It will be something to do. We don't have as much entertainment as you're used to in the city."

"That was kind of him. Yes, I will. I'll speak to him later today and see if I can arrange a suitable time to begin."

"And Maggie"—he paused in the doorway as he was leaving and gave her his wicked grin— "thank you for last night."

The old anger rushed to the surface. She was about to protest and to insist that he stop treating these disgraceful episodes as a joke when he added, "I mean, thank you for helping Mrs. Bateman with dinner. You made it a real success. Actually, Brenda was green with envy about the menu. She won't pay the wages for a really good cook herself, yet she's always furious when someone else serves better food."

With that, he was gone, and as usual, he had gotten the better of her.

Maggie swallowed the words she had been about to say and struggled to put her mind to the business of restoring the house. She must think of wallpaper and paint, of color schemes, furniture and fabric. And there was always the intriguing little puzzle of tracing the legend of Byron and Lady Caroline.

Chapter Four

For the next two days, Maggie saw little of Edan Deane. She caught a glimpse of him at breakfast, never saw him at lunch, had dinner with him briefly one night, and heard from Mrs. Bateman that he was dining with Brenda Hawke over at Chagford the next.

Furthermore, Peter didn't call. She knew he had been more than a little annoyed when he found Edan kissing her, but she could have explained it. She could have told him it meant nothing, if he had been nicer about it, if he hadn't dashed off like that. Kowtowing to the Duchess.

There was, however, plenty to keep her busy. She had Bateman bring down the satinwood chest. When it was cleaned up, she had a better opportunity to see it and discovered that it was a worthwhile find. The chairs, too, were worth reupholstering, once she decided on fabric. As for the commode, she intended to clean the ormolu herself as soon as she had time.

The second day after Peter's visit was terribly hot.

She worked in the library during the afternoon, going over papers that listed where certain pieces of Deane family furniture and carpets were stored. That would be part of her task in London—to find them and make arrangements to have them refurbished, cleaned, whatever was necessary. But of course, she would have to see them first and make up her mind how they could be used.

The day was sweltering. As late afternoon approached, it only seemed to get hotter and more humid. A storm must surely be brewing, she thought, but in the meantime the lake beckoned. She saw no sign of Edan and no one from the house ever went near the water. She decided to risk a swim and this time she would wear her bra and briefs. That was another thing she must do in London: pick up a couple of swimsuits. Having made up her mind, she took one of the large bath towels from her room and made her way over the hill to the water.

Inside the sauna hut, she undressed down to her underwear and draped the towel over her shoulders. Standing on the edge of the lake, she looked about but saw no one and, dropping the towel, plunged in. The water was fresh and sweet. She could not recall ever enjoying a swim more. How much nicer it was than a chlorinated pool!

The past two days had made her restless. Edan's advances had stirred up deep feelings, and Peter's discovery of that embrace in the moonlight might have upset him enough to alter their business relationship. Well, the only thing she could do now was try to keep Edan at bay and do a good job on the restoration of Deane Park. That was the professional attitude she must take.

The silken water, so cool and limpid, slid over her body in a sensuous way. It stirred up memories of Edan's kisses—by far the most intimate she had ever tasted. It was ridiculous to think how short a time they had known one another. But he was impossible. He was not a man any woman would find easy to live with, either. He wasn't ready to accept and encourage a wife's career, for one thing. She had realized that right from the beginning. He wanted a wife who would stay home and keep house; he was very old-fashioned.

She struck out strongly across the lake, feeling the need of exercise. Enough of dreaming; she needed action. When she had almost reached the far shore, she looked up to see Quinn on the ridge above the water. Poised on his horse like that, a silhouette against the orange sky, he looked for all the world like a painting. He waved at her and she acknowledged his greeting. She treaded water, waiting for him to walk down the sloping grass.

"Good afternoon, Miss Jordan," he said. "The water looks cool."

"Oh, it is, it's lovely. I was going to come over to the stables afterwards and talk to you about riding lessons. But now that you're here, perhaps we could settle it."

"Well, Miss, you can start tomorrow if you like. Early in the morning is best for me. Around six. Is that too soon?"

"No, I'm always awake out here in the country. It was quite a different matter in London, though."

The last rays of the sun caught her shoulders. Droplets trickled down her face, off the long lashes and tendrils of hair that clung to her cheeks.

Quinn said, "I'll see you tomorrow, then, Miss Jordan," and walked back up the hill to the spot where his horse was tethered.

That night at dinner, Edan didn't appear. She ate alone and afterwards retired to the library, where she put the small painting of the folly under the desk lamp in order to examine it. It was then that she made another exciting discovery. The dark-haired lover in the picture held a carnation in his hand! At first, its significance escaped her, but then she recalled reading a biography of Byron which reported that after their first meeting, Byron pursued Lady Caroline with an "exotic carnation." And right there in the painting was just such a flower—a carnation of palest pink. So pale, in fact, that when she had examined the picture earlier, she had failed to notice it. Surely this was another piece of evidence that Caroline, being such a romantic herself, would treasure the flower as a special sign of Byron's devotion.

As Maggie lay in bed that night, listening for sounds of Edan's car arriving home, she began to imagine his dinner and his evening with Brenda Hawke. Brenda was attractive, after all. And they probably thought they belonged together: they had the same interest in land, in horses and livestock, in servants, and in the restoration of their ancestral homes. They were, above all, born of the same class and trained to live the same kind of life. To them, Maggie was a stranger and a foreigner, though she had never considered herself one in London. Oh, what was the sense of thinking about it anyway? She didn't love Lord Deane. She certainly wouldn't marry a man of his type, who'd refuse to let her carry on with her career. He would be dominating. Demanding. She had always believed in freedom. And she believed that women had exactly the same right to live a full life as men.

Eventually, she fell asleep and never did find out what time Edan arrived home. But next morning she was certain it must have been quite late.

Despite her own restless night, she arrived at the stables shortly before six, wearing comfortable jeans and a T-shirt, ready for the lesson. Quinn was extremely polite and made no attempt to become too friendly.

They rode over trails worn through the grass on the Deane hills, along the stream and over the old stone bridge, and then around the perimeter of the estate.

At last, on a particularly high knoll, they paused to consider the view. Quinn pointed to a fairly large grove of trees in the distance, where she could see smoke rising.

"There's a gypsy encampment over there," he said.

"But is that allowed?"

"Yes, the gypsies have what you'd call 'squatters' rights.' I've lived with them most of my life, and so I'm used to seeing things from *their* side. We always camped on private property, usually as far away from the main buildings as possible."

"I don't think that's allowed at home, I mean in the United States," she said. "How do the gypsies make a living?"

"Oh, in different ways. Sometimes they hunt for animals and fish. They sell things, they mend things, they tell fortunes. One of the things they do best is buy and sell horses."

"That's what Lord Deane said."

She could not help feeling there was an air of adventure about the word "gypsy," about the freedom of their life.

"Do they know you work here, Quinn?"

"Sure, they know. It's the band I was with. I visited over there last night. They wonder why I left that life and why I want to work regular hours, I suppose."

"Well, I think you're right. It must give you more security, a job like this one," she encouraged.

"That's what *I* think, Miss Jordan. But you know, my friends over at the camp think I'll soon miss the moving about, the change of scene, the close friendships. You always have friends when you're part of a band like that. They help each other. You can depend on them."

When her lesson was over, Maggie changed into fresh clothes and brought out the house plans once more. This time she concentrated on the drawings for the folly. It would be a good idea to see whether the Finns, who had rented the property at one time, had changed the design, or if they had left it in the original state.

The morning had darkened. In the east, clouds were forming into grey cotton mountains. The air was heavy with moisture and there were distant rumblings of thunder. "No swim today," she told herself, "there's a storm coming."

Nevertheless, she was drawn across the lawns to the folly, which she unlocked with the keys Edan Deane had given her. Then she sat in the very center of the floor and tried to absorb the mood of the place. She could hear the storm getting closer, and all around, from the windows on every side, she watched the clouds gather and spread, deepening from grey to black. Great bolts of lightning, followed by a pause and then a rumbling, gave notice of the speed with which the storm was approaching the park.

She wondered if she would be safe in the little frame building. But, on the other hand, it had already stood there a long time, and so far lightning had apparently missed it. Should she make a run for the house or wait out the storm in the folly? Before she could make up her mind, the rain spattered down in huge, fat drops, the door flew open, and Edan came in, shaking water off his hair and slamming the door behind him. The rain had turned into a solid sheet.

"Fate has brought us together once again, Miss Jordan," he said, giving her one of his devastating smiles. "My, my, how I wish there were a fireplace in this hideaway. Wouldn't a fire be your wish, if you had a genie in a bottle?"

"My wish would be more along the lines of solitude,"

she said icily. How dare he spend half of last night with
Brenda Hawke, and then come in here and pretend to
be delighted to see her?

"Not in a storm," he said. "In a storm, a lady wants
some protection."

"I'm much more likely to need protection from *you*,"
she pointed out, "judging from past experience."

"Boys will be boys, you know. Or did somebody say
that already? Now, let me see. In this window seat,
there ought to be a bottle of schnapps. A habit I picked
up from the former Finnish tenants. Yes, here it is. And
glasses, too."

He produced a bottle of clear white liquor, along
with two glasses, as if he were a magician producing
rabbits from a hat.

The thunder drowned his next words. Maggie
jumped. Although she wasn't especially afraid of
storms, this one seemed very close. The rain was so
solid now, nothing could be seen out of the windows. It
was like being in a shower without getting wet. Rain
was all around them and there were sudden sharp
illuminations of lightning that zigzagged to the earth.
The panes of glass trembled.

"Here we are," Edan said, handing her the
schnapps. "Drink that. It'll steady your nerves."

"My nerves are perfectly steady."

Unfortunately, that wasn't true. As she took the
glass, her hand shook—whether from the storm or from
Edan's nearness, she could not be sure. She tasted the
drink, which was terribly strong and dry.

"Uugh. That's awful-tasting stuff."

"Better than nothing. It'll warm you."

"I don't need warming, thank you."

"Ah, but you *do*, Miss Jordan. There are times, such
as now, when you strike me as being very cold. For
example, look at our situation. Here we are, two
people stranded in a delightful, romantic little building.

Like Byron and Caro. And you're on one side and I'm on the other. Nothing very warm about that, is there?"

"It suits *me,* Lord Deane. It suits me fine. Now, if your dear Brenda were here, it would be quite another matter. Then you could be as romantic as you like."

"So that's it? You're jealous of Brenda! Well, she's lovely to look at, I'll admit."

"Lovely enough to spend half the night with."

He gave her a veiled look. "That's my affair."

"I'm sure it *is* an affair. That's my point. It's your life, so keep it to yourself. And keep your hands off me."

"They aren't on you . . . not yet."

With that, he emptied the glass and quickly refilled it. Then he came closer. He was just about to put his arms around her when a horrendous bolt of lightning pierced the oak trees just outside the door. There was a deafening crack, a blue flame. The folly shook.

She leaped toward him, so startled that she had no time to think. He wrapped his arms around her, pulling her close. She buried her face in his neck. As if she suddenly realized what she had done, that she had encouraged such intimacy, she pulled herself free.

The room was dark as night after the lightning, and her face was starkly white, her eyes huge. She stared up at him from the honey cloud of hair. In the tight white T-shirt, each breast was shadowed in the very center and so enticing it drew him toward her again. He covered her mouth with his own, his lips seeking and hungry. Her bare arms circled his neck, her fingers searched his nape where the black hair grew long and dark. He groaned. And they collapsed to the floor, in a tangle of warm flesh.

A cold splash of water split the dream. Drops touched the back of her hand, where it clasped his shoulder, and dribbled down toward Edan's arm, and she saw another touch his cheek.

Edan leaped up this time, swearing.

"The roof's leaking!" he cried. "That tree landed right on the folly!"

They both began to laugh. There was nothing else to do. Edan Deane poured them each another schnapps and they waited out the storm sitting on the floor. But Maggie knew that she must be careful from now on. She had skated too near the edge to feel safe ever again. Her behavior was appalling. Her heart still thumped and her stomach still shuddered with the need, the urgency of this man's kisses.

When the storm was over and they walked through the wet grass toward the house, she said, "That was my fault. The lightning scared me. I'm sorry, Edan, I won't do that again."

"My pleasure," he said. "Please, do it again. Anytime you wish."

"You know what I mean. It's—well, it's dangerous. It leads to things I don't feel I can handle. I don't know what it is about you that makes me act this way. This job *is* important to me, and I want to do well—I guess that's why I'm nervous."

"You're talking a lot of rot, but if you want to believe it, that's fine with me," Edan said, opening the door for her. "Let's have lunch, then there's something I must do on the far side of the estate. And now, I'll have to arrange for the roof on the folly to be fixed. There's always something waiting to be done. It never ends."

They talked little during lunch. Only about safe subjects: the weather, repairing the folly, and whether or not Maggie could clean up the commode herself or whether she needed professional help. Edan had seen it after Bateman brought it downstairs for examination.

"I know how to polish ormolu," she said. "So I'll try to do it myself. If Mrs. Bateman has some ammonia."

Edan left soon after lunch, and she settled to work on the cabinet in an unused sitting room. She had read that the trick was to unscrew the tiny brass carvings and scrub them in ammonia to remove traces of oxidation. Then, after pouring boiling water over them, and letting them dry quickly so no moisture remained to turn them green, they would glitter like gold.

Maggie worked hard all afternoon and was so absorbed in her task that she forgot to look at the clock. She had scarcely enough time to bathe and change for dinner, and when she arrived in the dining room, Edan was waiting.

"Did you know we have gypsies in the park?" he asked when she was seated.

"Quinn told me this morning. The band he lived with, apparently. You know, Edan, I'm convinced he wants to settle down here and work for you. But he misses his friends."

"I suppose he does. Being with a band of gypsies must be like living with a houseful of aunts and uncles. There's always somebody around to give advice, to help out, to talk to."

"I wouldn't know. I was an only child. And I have only one aunt and she moved to the West Coast."

"You missed a great deal. Would you like to go over to the camp after dinner? Quinn suggested we might like to meet them. They may sing for us, or even offer to tell your fortune. You women like that sort of thing, don't you?"

"And I suppose *men* never have their fortunes told?"

"Don't get huffy about it. It was only a joke."

"I'd love to go if you're sure you can behave," she said primly.

Edan laughed.

"You have my word, Miss Jordan. My solemn oath as a gentleman and a farmer. And as a Lord of the Realm. But the grass will be wet, so wear gum boots."

"Thank you. I thought of that."

"In my own defence, I must say it's partly your fault

I've behaved like that. You shouldn't be so attractive. You can't blame me entirely, you know."

She could have argued the point but thought better of it. Since he had already given his word, she would accept it. If he broke it tonight, then there would be no more walks in the evening with Lord Deane.

The storm had cooled the air, and the world was mint-fresh. A gentle breeze rustled through the great trees and as they walked by the stream, Maggie could hear it rippling over rocks underneath the willows. Deane Park was a beautiful spot, almost as untouched as it had been in the days when Lady Caroline ran laughing through the gardens.

Long before they saw anyone, they heard sounds from the camp. There was a smell of smoke in the air, mixed with cooking meat. As they drew near, they could hear a guitar and a man singing a sad song.

When they pushed through the cedar grove, they came upon the cluster of wagons and tents. A huge bonfire burned on a patch of bare earth, giving a reddish light to the faces, so that it looked like an enormous stage set. They could see Quinn talking with a small, dark girl wearing a bright red scarf around her hair.

Quinn spotted them and came over.

"Good evening, Milord, Miss Jordan. Would you like to meet some of my friends?"

"Of course, Quinn. That's why we came."

They met a number of people, including the pretty girl Quinn had been chatting with when they arrived.

"Meta," he said, "would you tell Miss Jordan's fortune? Meta reads palms. She's very good."

"If you like," the girl said softly. "Come sit over here, Miss."

She took Maggie's left hand in hers and turned it over. Then, after examining the other hand, too, she said, "There is a strange woman in your life, very beautiful, but perhaps—perhaps a bit mad. She dances around you, you cannot seem to pin her down—she is very important to you—yet it is hard to see her, hard to understand her—"

"Yes, yes," Maggie cried excitedly. "You see, Edan? That's Lady Caroline. Yes, that's who it is."

"Oh," he said, with a tinge of sarcasm. "I thought it might be Brenda Hawke."

"Brenda Hawke isn't important to me. Why would she appear in my fortune? Go on, please. *Do* go on!"

The girl continued to study her palm. Slowly she added, "As well as the woman, the beautiful woman, there is a handsome man. Dark. Important. Sensitive."

"You see? That's Byron!" Maggie said happily. "Oh, I'm sure it's all going to work out."

"I thought the man might be me," Edan said, grinning at her in that special way he had. "Why would you think of Lord Byron when Lord Deane is standing right beside you?"

"Because," Maggie said, flashing him a warning look, "Byron is important to my work. And he fits the description. I'd hardly call *you* sensitive!"

"Now *that* was uncalled for, Miss Jordan," Edan said and strolled away with Quinn to discuss something concerning the horses.

When she tried to pay Meta, the girl refused. It was, she said calmly, not a very clear fortune. Some other time, perhaps, it would be possible to tell more, but not tonight.

On the way home, Edan was cool. So cool that Maggie was afraid she had really offended him. Perhaps she ought not to have been so blunt. He did not even coax her to have a nightcap with him in the library, and she went off to bed feeling strangely dissatisfied. Yet why was she complaining? He had kept his word. And that was what she had wished.

Chapter Five

The next day the gypsies moved on and it was only when Brenda Hawke called to complain to Edan that they had moved onto her property that they found out. However, since Brenda was going to London anyway—"I have a meeting with my lawyer, Trevithick, about expenses"—she supposed it shouldn't matter to her where the gypsies camped.

Maggie had decided to drive into London also. She needed more clothes and she was anxious to see the carpets and antiques that were stored. She would have to make an important decision about the carpet for the First Drawing Room before she could decide on a color scheme. But the most important thing was the painting. She was anxious to authenticate it. To prove to Brenda Hawke that she was wrong, that Lord Byron and Lady Caroline had definitely stayed in Deane Park and that it was not just a myth but a beautiful and romantic interlude.

By midafternoon, she had arrived at her elegant little

office tucked away in Mount Street. After checking the appointment calendar and the mail, she put in a call to Peter at Elwyn House. After some delay he was finally located and brought to the telephone.

"Peter, how are you? I'm in the office. Is there any chance you can come in for dinner tonight? I'd like to go over some of my ideas with you."

"Ah, you escaped the pastoral scene, then?"

She detected a hint of sarcasm in Peter's voice. Still, he sounded a bit friendlier than he had at Deane Park.

"There was no escape. I come and go as I please. At any rate, I brought the painting along. And I'm going over to the warehouse tomorrow morning to take a look at the carpets and furniture in storage. But there are some points I'd very much like to discuss with you. Can you possibly drive into town?"

"Not tonight, I'm afraid. The Duchess and I are dining up the road at Ecclestone. It's a house I've wanted to see for years. Pure Elizabethan. Absolutely perfect condition. So I can't pass up the chance."

"Oh." She thought of dining alone and felt a bit of a letdown. "Well, shall I ask Everly Jones to take a look at the picture? Will he be the best person, do you think?"

Everly was employed at the Royal Academy as a restorer. He was a recognized expert in British paintings of the last three centuries. And if he could not identify the artist himself, he would be able to suggest other ways in which it could be done.

"Right, he's your best bet. Call him right away and ask for an appointment tomorrow. He'll be fascinated, anyway, by your little find. I can come by and pick you up at his studio around noon and we'll lunch at San Stefano's."

"All right, Peter, that's what I'll do. Unless you hear from me to cancel, come to Burlington House around twelve."

"You'd better reserve for lunch," Peter said. "You know Bunny freezes everyone out if they have no reservation."

Bunny was the eccentric proprietor of San Stefano's, a chic restaurant on Beauchamp Place. Her house rules were erratic but if she happened to take it into her tousled head to kiss a guest upon the cheek, it was a sign of recognition and a good table was assured. A table at the hub of things was essential since it was one of those eateries where everyone came to see and be seen.

"I'll do that. Talk to you tomorrow."

She felt better, having spoken to Peter. At least he wasn't angry, and it would give her confidence to go ahead with her plans for Deane Park if she could hash over some of the ideas with him. Next, she put in a call to Everly and he readily agreed to appraise the painting. Her third call, to the warehouse, assured her of an afternoon appointment there. The Deane furniture hadn't been examined by the family for some time. Carpets would have to be unrolled and dust sheets removed so that she could properly assess what was stored.

At last, when it was nearly six, she felt free to seek refuge in her own flat. Through Peter, she had been lucky enough to rent, very cheaply, part of a townhouse on Cheyne Walk. The owner spent most of the year in Switzerland and was glad to have a custodian who could be relied upon. He reserved the bottom floor for his own use, and Maggie used the top two floors.

She had always found the house, which had a historic past, to be warm and inviting. Tonight, looking out over the Thames from the dining-room window, she could see the fairy lights of Chelsea Bridge and the boats and barges plying the river.

Behind her were the moss-green panelling, the carefully chosen Egyptian-style prints, and the dark wood of the Jacobean sideboard and refectory table. She had lighted the candles in two tall brass holders.

But somehow that familiar feeling of "belonging" failed to materialize. The rooms were filled with pieces of furniture of her own choosing and pictures she had bought. The colors, the fabrics were a reflection of her own taste. Still, she felt lonely and a bit out of place. Well, she would try music. She put on a recording of Handel's *Water Music*. That had always soothed her in the past and was a perfect complement to the view of the Thames.

Even Handel did not produce his usual magic. She still felt restless, wanting something, wanting to be somewhere else. But she could not analyze it. What on earth was the matter with her? Everything was going smoothly.

In the kitchen, she made a pot of coffee. Then she propped the painting on a dining-room chair under a light and studied it. The two pale lovers sat there rather mistily, completely out of time and place. They were awkwardly drawn, but the artist had managed to catch a feeling of adoration, of devotion, of complete absorption between the two people, just the same. The scene drew her mind to Deane Park. What was Edan doing? And Quinn? And was the folly roof being repaired properly?

She caught herself in these thoughts and felt angry. She was behaving just as if Deane Park belonged to her! Which was ridiculous. Edan Deane was an intolerable man. She certainly didn't want him. Let him have Brenda Hawke, a union he seemed to be considering, if you counted all the time he spent with the woman. She, Maggie, would go back and do her job. Try to restore the house to its former beauty. That was what she was

being paid to do. That, and nothing else. Still, it would
be nice to go back. The house had the power to
enchant, no use arguing with that.

She would read, she decided. Try to finish the travel
book on India that she had found so fascinating before
she had gone to Deane Park. Her mind wandered. She
wanted to read some Byron; that was what she really
needed now. Quickly she pulled out the leather-bound
volume of *Don Juan* that Peter had given her. Opening
it at random, she read:

> 'Tis sweet to hear the watchdog's honest bark
> Bay deep-mouth'd welcome as we draw near
> home:
> 'Tis sweet to know there is an eye will mark
> Our coming, and look brighter when we come.

Oh, what was the use? She snapped the book shut
and began to pace before the window, looking alter-
nately at the river and at the painting as it sat upon the
chair. Finally she went to bed, but it was not a restful
sleep.

In the morning, she drove straight to Burlington
House, with the painting on the seat beside her. She
felt a sense of excitement, as if she were unravelling
some important mystery, instead of merely identifying
a small, insignificant painting.

Everly Jones was friendly and enthusiastic. The
painting, he said, could easily be one of Caroline's. He
looked up material in a book he had already taken out
of the files. It contained a reproduction of one of Lady
Caroline's small paintings and a photograph of her
signature.

"You see, it is very similar, the way she's signed it,"
Everly said, picking up the picture again. "The next
step is actually to see one of her known paintings and
compare the style. And the signature, too."

"Do you know where we can find one?"

"Yes, I'm sure I do. If you leave the picture with me, I'll arrange things. We'll have it dated at the same time. The whole thing will take a couple of weeks, depending on luck."

"Do you think I'm being foolish? That I'm making too much of the coincidence—the stories about the lovers being at Deane Park and then the picture?"

"Certainly not! You're quite right to pursue it. What a nice touch if it really is Caroline's picture! You can hang it in the house. And that commode you describe sounds like a jewel."

"I'm taking it to a furniture dealer we work with often," she assured him. "But I thought it best to begin with the painting. It seems more important."

When Peter arrived, he made light of her project, but at the same time he was warmer toward her than he had been in the country. He kissed her cheek and handed her a bunch of violets he had bought on the street.

"Here, my romantic friend. I'm not Byron, I'm afraid, not even the fascinating Lord Deane. But you'll have to make do with me over lunch. Are we set for San Stefano's?"

"Yes, we have a table. Thank you for the flowers, Peter, it was sweet of you." She decided to ignore his reference to Edan.

She pinned the flowers to her dress, thinking Peter was kind and thoughtful. He had been considerate and helpful ever since she first met him. If he was slightly annoyed over her behavior out on the estate, one could hardly blame him.

Everly Jones promised to look after the picture and call her in a week or so to report on his detective work. He followed them out into the sunshine and watched while Peter hailed a cab to take them to Beauchamp Place.

"You found the right man," Peter said, patting her hand. "He'll find out if anyone can. Now, forget about the painting for a while and let's talk about your plans for Deane Park."

The door at San Stefano's was narrow: so narrow it was difficult to find. So typical of London, Maggie thought, where some of the best eating places were carefully hidden. Finding them was supposed to be half the fun.

They navigated a steep flight of stairs that might have passed for a goat track and wound up in a tiny bar decorated with fresh pink roses and an enormous portrait of Chou En-lai. A skylight over the main dining area and a jungle of green plants made it look like a greenhouse.

At one o'clock, the right time to lunch, it was filled with exquisitely tailored men accompanying women wearing designer jeans and silk blouses hung with gold chains. Among them were celebrities, titled people, and some who were just plain rich. The service was always desultory, but no one seemed to mind: bottles of house wine were planted like trees upon the tables and waiters made no attempt to pour. The use of toothbrush glasses instead of stemware implied a bizarre form of "roughing it."

No matter what the whims of the proprietor happened to be, the food was always excellent. That was a cardinal rule of the fashionable restaurants. The décor might be wild, but the food was delicious. The fettuccine was as delicate as the waiters were sulky, and the mushrooms soaked in wine, the tender veal, could always be relied upon.

Maggie had always loved coming here. Peter knew many people and could point them out and tell her bits of gossip. Today, however, she had lost her enthusiasm. The other customers looked brittle and bored. She felt no curiosity about the Marchioness sitting at the next table with her two daughters, both wearing tweed hacking jackets with elbow patches edged in brilliants.

"She's husband-hunting for those two," Peter whispered.

And when he nodded to a well-known actor across the room, lunching with a former racing-car driver who had just missed winning the Grand Prix the year before by seconds, she scarcely looked.

If Peter noticed her preoccupation, he did not comment. After lunch they parted, he to go shopping for fabrics needed at Elwyn House, she to keep an appointment at the warehouse to view the belongings of Lord Deane's ancestors.

She selected a fine Aubusson, a huge carpet in warm beiges and rusts that would be perfect for the First Drawing Room. On today's market it would cost a fortune, so it was wise to use the rug as a focal point. She chose several pieces of furniture and a number of carpets and directed them to be sent to Deane Park. The collection of *famille rose* dishes would look well in the small breakfast room, for right from the beginning she had visualized a corner cabinet filled with china.

Once she had completed her task at the warehouse, she was anxious to get home. She felt dusty and hot and eager to take a leisurely bath and change for her evening date with Peter. He had bought tickets to a play at the Savoy Theatre, and when they arrived the lights were still up. The Savoy was an intimate, though slightly shabby, theatre with a feeling of comfort and tradition. Maggie had counted it as a favorite because of its welcoming atmosphere.

They had just taken their seats when she caught sight of Edan's head several rows ahead. And there beside him sat Brenda Hawke! Her heart sloughed downward with alarming speed.

So he had followed Brenda Hawke to London! Was he so desperate to see the woman that he couldn't remain in the country? Well, she had known the two were close, that had been evident when she arrived. And he'd never stopped seeing Brenda, either. Brenda herself had indicated quite clearly that she regarded Edan as her own property. There was nothing new in all this and no need for Maggie to feel so disappointed at the sight of them together.

Despite her lectures to herself, Maggie scarcely heard a word that was said upon the stage. On the drive home to Cheyne Walk, she was silent. When she did not invite Peter in for a drink, he looked a bit downcast but did not argue.

"I'll drive back to Elwyn House tonight," he said as he kissed her on the cheek. "The Duchess will be happier if I'm there for breakfast. Poor darling, she gets lonely."

"You can be there in a hour if you leave right away," Maggie said vaguely.

To her, the Duchess was a mythical figure. Since they had never met she could not even imagine the woman, and the Duchess's problems did not rate any serious consideration. Her mind revolved around Edan's being here in London with Brenda. Even now, they might be having a romantic late-night drink in some cosy spot, and Edan might be holding Brenda's hand and whispering loving things in her ear. And perhaps kissing her. And then—

She could not bear to continue that line of thought. Once she was safely in her flat she began to pace around. She played music that should have soothed her. Music that ordinarily would have made her feel good inside. When had Mozart failed to please? But tonight it did no good whatsoever. She did not want food or a drink—she didn't even want to sleep.

Visions of Deane Park kept drifting through her

mind. The pinkish stone of the house, the graceful windows, the huge trees, the exquisite little folly. The folly. Had the roof been repaired? If not, and it rained again, the floor would be damaged. Edan was in London, and obviously he wouldn't be there to do anything if such a catastrophe occurred.

Since she couldn't sleep, she might as well do something useful. It would be easy enough to drive back to Deane Park tonight. Then, if there was a storm, she could supervise repairs, see that no more serious damage was done to the folly. In that way, she would be on hand to begin work first thing in the morning, too. So, when she considered every angle, returning tonight was the sensible thing to do.

It was one-thirty in the morning when at last she drove through the stone gates and along the silent, narrow road that led to the house. There was no storm. Not a sign of rain, in fact, and scarcely a cloud in the sky.

When she drew up before the front door, she was surprised to see Edan's Mercedes. He must have been a mere few minutes ahead, she thought, because the headlights were still on. And on the gravel drive, beside the car, was Edan himself. There was no sign of Brenda Hawke.

Chapter Six

As she brought the Morris to a stop, she saw Edan turn off his own car lights and walk toward her.

"Well, well, well. If it isn't Miss Jordan! What are *you* doing back so soon? I thought you were planning to spend a couple of days in the city."

The husky quality of his voice, now so devastatingly familiar, sent a shock wave through her body and suggested there might be other, deeper reasons why she had come back early. Reasons which had nothing to do with repairs to the folly roof. Under his searching gaze, she became aware of her blown hair and lack of lipstick. Suddenly these things became important.

"I might ask you the same question," she managed to say. "When I left Deane Park you didn't mention a trip to London."

"How did you know I was in London?"

His tone was sharp. As if he thought she might be spying on him. The hint of amusement had vanished. Well, she would soon correct *that* impression!

"Purely by accident, I assure you. It's of no interest to me what you do."

"Isn't it? You're right, I did drive in to London. Something came up. Unexpectedly."

"A call from Miss Hawke, perhaps? Saying she had tickets to the theatre?"

"So you were at the Savoy!" He opened the car door for her but his words were icy. "I didn't see you."

"I'm not surprised. You spent all your time looking at Miss Hawke."

He made no reply to this. Instead, he brought out his keys and unlocked the front door. Maggie followed him, wishing she had not been so talkative. She ought not to have let him know she had even noticed him at the theatre. What a silly mistake *that* was.

Inside, Bateman had left on a small night light. As Edan put the bolt on the door, Maggie paused at the foot of the stairs, now in shadow. The house was so still that every move she made, even her breathing, seemed unnaturally loud.

"Did you go to the theatre with Peter?"

"Yes, I did. He drove in from Elwyn House especially to consult with me. I wanted his opinion on my plans. He also suggested that I take the painting to one of the restorers at the Royal Academy. It's being appraised right now."

"So it was all business then?"

"Yes, it was all business. You ought to be pleased. Isn't that exactly what you wanted? Peter Cross's views on how Deane Park should be restored?"

Edan seemed to back down a little.

"It isn't that I don't value *your* ideas—it's just that Peter has so much more experience."

"I see. Well, now you've got what you want."

They still had not moved from the foot of the stairs. He seemed to have something else on his mind.

"Not that it's any of your business, Miss Jordan, but I

was having a business meeting with Brenda. I just bought ten acres of pasture from her. It's a bit of her property that juts right into mine, so it seemed sensible for me to take it over. Her lawyer had the papers ready and I went in to the city to sign them. The theatre was only an afterthought."

"I'm sorry. I shouldn't have spoken like that."

They were still standing in the darkness, as if they had suddenly been rooted on the hall carpet. Beside her, Edan loomed very large. They were speaking in half-whispers, unconsciously trying not to disturb the quiet of the house.

"Anyway, if you had a date with Peter, why did you drive back in the middle of the night? That strikes me as peculiar. Did you two have an argument?"

"Nothing like that. As a matter of fact, he wanted to get back to Elwyn House, and I was restless when I got to my flat. I just couldn't seem to settle down. I don't usually feel that way. I love London. But I began to think about the work to be done here at Deane Park, and the chance of another rainstorm ruining the folly before the repairs could be completed—well, I got so concerned I drove back."

"You were worried about Deane Park?"

"I couldn't help it. I guess I just have a habit of getting involved in my work."

He laughed softly.

"You're a funny girl."

She thought he was going to touch her, to renew that intimacy which she had always found so upsetting. He leaned down toward her, and she could see the brilliant eyes in the shadows of the hall. However, he drew back.

"You must be tired," was all he said.

In her room, Maggie found that Mrs. Bateman had left the window open. Tonight there was a pleasant breeze, and the air was fresh and invigorating after the city. She had washed and put on a nightgown and was just about to climb into bed when she heard a tap at the door. Without waiting for an answer, Edan came in. He closed the door behind him.

"You're not asleep yet, I hope? I'm sorry I was so inhospitable. When a lady drives all the way from London just to watch over my property, the least I can do is offer her a nightcap."

He had a tray, on which there were two glasses of a dark-red wine.

"Port," he said. "Will you have a glass?"

"Well, all right."

She had left on a small light with a pink bulb and shade. Its dim glow scarcely made a dent in the darkness. But she was grateful for the subdued light, since her nightgown offered little protection. The lace bodice revealed far too much of her breasts—the firm, tilted shape of them, the dark tips. And the skirt clung to her hips and thighs.

"I wasn't expecting you to come. I mean, I was just getting into bed," she began defensively, as she took the wine, setting it on the table.

He set his own glass down untouched.

"Maggie," he began hoarsely, "you have the wildest effect on me. . . . I can't seem to help myself."

His arms reached out to her, and automatically she went toward him. Not by choice. Not by reason. Directed only by her senses. In the tight circle of his embrace, held so close to him, she felt cosseted and pampered as she had never felt before. Safe and warm and, at the same time, strangely excited. As if anything were possible. As if anything were permissible.

Her long, thick, honey-colored hair flowed against his, so dark and shaggy. Her cheek pressed against the roughness of his. The last traces of a musky male scent still lingered on his skin. His hands felt large and capable, strong on her shoulders. They slid down to her narrow waist, down to her hips as he pulled her against his urgent maleness.

Common sense fled. He picked her up as if she weighed nothing and placed her on the bed. Then he stood gazing down at her hungrily as she lay there in the flimsy gown. As their eyes met, she caught the pent-up energy that was poised like a hawk to swoop down upon her. She trembled but made no move to escape.

Instead, she was paralyzed by his terrible need. It overwhelmed her in the same way that his mouth had overwhelmed her mouth, and in the same way that his body now covered her body. For a moment, she sank into a blissful sea of surrender, stirred with a mad desire she had never felt before. Her own fancies flooded every nerve, every corner of her mind.

Edan groaned. He took her in his arms again and his mouth conducted a search that began with her eyelids and traveled over her face and neck. She remembered that morning in the sauna when he had seen her completely naked, and she knew that here in the mysterious shadows his tongue would soon discover what his eyes already knew.

"I need you, Maggie . . ." he murmured in her ear. "I want you, how I want you—oh, Maggie . . ."

"Edan, Edan," she whispered.

She wanted to yield to him, to make him a gift of her body. She was on the verge of total surrender; every nerve was stretched to breaking, every secret longing was crying for fulfillment. Then, without warning, he lifted himself away from her and stood up. For a long moment he looked down at her. She had never seen such desperation, such hunger in a man's eyes. But when he spoke, his voice was sad and touched with gentleness.

"What am I doing? Maggie, what am I doing to you? To us?"

She began to shake. She realized that a cool, invisible

barrier had risen between them. And yet, only moments ago, she had been willing to give him everything. She had been willing to taste the ultimate joy. With a trembling hand, she pulled the quilt over her bare shoulders and turned her head into the pillow. As she heard his footsteps retreating, the tears started. Edan opened the door and then closed it firmly. She did not even look, but she knew, with some regret, that he might well be closing the door on an episode of her life. Yet, if Edan hadn't been strong, they might have embarked upon a course that would have ruined them both.

Although she was exhausted emotionally, she still got up at six the next morning and walked over to the stables to find Quinn. As it happened, he was free to give her a lesson and she was pleased to have something to absorb her attention. It was a bright, glowing morning and they took a trail in the direction of the old gardener's cottage. As they came to the gate, they could see Farraday already out weeding his garden.

He ambled over to the gate to greet them.

"Nice morning, Miss. Would you like to see the new pups?"

"Oh, yes, I certainly would."

She was glad of an excuse to dismount. She felt stiff, and her energy had ebbed since she first began the lesson. While she admired the German shepherd puppies, Farraday pointed out one in particular.

"Now that one, Miss, is special. He's intelligent, that one."

She laughed. The dogs seemed too young to show any signs of personality. But she had to admit that the pup he selected looked up at her in a rather precocious way.

"He *is* different, Mister Farraday," she admitted.

"Ah yes, I'll keep me eye on *that* one!"

On the way back to the stables, Quinn offered her the news that he was going to Newmarket with Lord Deane that morning to buy additional horses.

"He wants my opinion," Quinn said, obviously pleased.

"That's wonderful. I'm glad you're getting on so well."

She felt oddly disappointed, though, that Edan hadn't even mentioned the horse fair. Well, she couldn't expect him to invite her, after all. She was here to work, not to go off on jaunts around the countryside, and anyway she knew nothing about horses.

But it was with a sharp pang of something she preferred to think of as surprise, rather than jealousy, that she noticed Brenda Hawke's car arrive around ten o'clock. And when Edan's Mercedes drove off, Brenda was in the front with him and Quinn was in the back. She reminded herself that Brenda knew a great deal about horses. It was natural that Edan would invite her along. Yet when she recalled last night, and how close she had come to surrendering, she flushed hotly with anger and resentment at Edan's behavior. No doubt he treated Brenda Hawke like some precious ornament. He wouldn't dare try to push *her* around.

During the following week, she saw little of Edan Deane. Both made a point of keeping out of the other's way. Even at meal times, Maggie seldom found herself in Edan's company. The estate absorbed most of his attention. There was the folly roof to supervise, the fences to alter since he'd bought the pasture from Brenda, and his consultations with a plumbing contractor. All the pipes in Deane Park were antiquated and had to be replaced if more bathrooms were to be used.

Quinn was settling in well, too, although sometimes during the riding lessons, Maggie noticed that he seemed worried. She didn't ask what was troubling him because she felt it would be wrong to intrude, but something obviously was wrong. In any event, she had plenty to keep her busy. At times she wondered if she could handle the whole thing herself. She often thought of telephoning Peter and asking his advice, but since her visit to London he had chosen to ignore her. *Both* men were apparently capable of ignoring her, she decided, so she'd do exactly the same.

Her overall plan called for redecoration of the First Drawing Room and the library immediately. The drawing room would be the flagship, setting the style for the entire project. The library, which Edan often used, would be cosier. Everyone, she reasoned, needed a haven where they could either relax or work in peace. She wanted to brighten the room, use stronger colors, and put in more comfortable furniture.

She hired a platoon of floor cleaners and wood scrapers to begin, but when Edan complained that he had lost the use of the library, she was forced to decide on a quick substitute. Considering the available rooms, she fastened on the "rent room." It had caught her fancy on that moonlight night, almost two weeks before, but she had never explored it in detail. Now she had the carpet cleaned and a few pieces of furniture brought in from other rooms to make it habitable. The fireplace worked, which would be a blessing during the evening when the weather turned damp.

A maroon carpet was laid from wall to wall, except for an alcove in one corner. There the floor was left bare. The seasoned oak had darkened with age, which was to be expected, but why was the alcove floor about three inches higher than the rest of the room? It made no sense. Such a small space could not possibly conceal a passage or a closet.

The puzzle bothered her, and the next time she and Edan dined together, she confronted him.

"Do you remember any family stories about the rent

room? Anything that might explain that difference in the floor level? I can't find a clue in the original plans you gave me."

"I didn't know there *was* a difference in the floor level," Edan said. "We haven't used the room for years."

"Well, the alcove is a bit higher than the rest of the room."

"Is it? I'll take a look. But as for stories . . . I suppose you're thinking of a secret passage or something? The only mystery I recall about the house was the priest hole. There's supposed to be one in Deane Park, but I don't know where the opening is."

Priest holes were a feature of many English country houses. They had been the entrances to tunnels leading to a concealed place off the property. Whenever there had been religious persecution, priests had been smuggled to safety by sympathizers.

"A priest hole? That's marvellous! Why didn't you tell me before? We might find it during the restoration," Maggie said excitedly.

Edan smiled at her enthusiasm, but he was a realist. "If we did come across a priest hole, the tunnel would have caved in by now, Maggie, and it could be dangerous. I wouldn't spend money to have it dug out. What would be the use?"

Maggie knew he was quite correct. There would be no point in opening up what would probably turn out to be a nuisance.

In the next weeks, she added to her list of fabrics and wallpapers, of furniture and carpets. She made many a raid upon the attic, and during one of them she pulled out the harp from inside its dusty cover, that she had seen in the room with the commode. It needed new strings and she wasn't at all sure it was worth bringing downstairs. But when Bateman delivered it to her in the front hall for closer inspection, she found a signature: "Erard." A bit of quick research revealed that since it had a double pedal, it was certainly made after 1810. Now who had gone to all the trouble of importing a harp? Had a family chatelaine, one of the earlier Deane women, been musical?

She sent the harp to London to be restrung and tuned. It was the harp, really, that drove her to search the dusty trunks for letters or bills of sale. She would like to establish who had bought it, and why. Every afternoon, after the workmen had disappeared, she spent an hour in the attic boxes and trunks, looking for information about the harp.

And eventually she was rewarded. For in a sea chest—one of the Deanes had obviously been a sailor—she found a faded brown book. The title page was headed "The Journal of Lady Amalie Deane—1809." The script was graceful, fragile but flowing. Maggie leafed through it quickly, to pick up some hint of the style, and soon found that while Lady Amalie was restless, she was also something of a hostess—and a musician—who longed for a "goode pianoforte." Or a "harp." Maggie set down the book and continued the search; volumes for the years 1811 and 1812 turned up in the sea chest as well.

This was more like it. She took all the journals down with her and resolved to read them carefully in good light. The faded handwriting was not easily translated, but she felt it would be worthwhile. Here, then, might lie some reference not only to the purchase of the harp and who had played it, but the names of guests. And if so, there was a chance that Lady Caroline's name would appear. Maggie felt as if she had unearthed a treasure. She decided, however, not to mention the find to Edan until she had some information that would be valuable.

Three days later she had still found no reference to

Lady Caroline, a marked disappointment. One mention of a harp bought in London excited her. Lady Amalie wrote she was "having a devlish time getting it forwarded to the Park." She also referred to a "priest hole with a fairely dry tunnel—which leads, I believe, to some cedars by the stream. A man of resolve could crawl along it safely—a lover would find it a pretty escape."

Lady Amalie did not confess whether or not she ever found a lover of resolve who would use the priest hole as a tunnel, but she went on to say that "no doubt it was made to save some priests when Henry was on his rampage against the Catholicks." Meaning, Maggie supposed, Henry the Eighth and his Reformation, when priests had been hounded from abbeys and monasteries and, in many cases, murdered.

Shortly after this discovery, she again confronted Edan with evidence of his family history. This time, he was ensconced in the rent room. He had become quite accustomed to using it by now and didn't appear to miss the library at all. He offered her a sherry.

"I've been reading some journals written by one of your ancestors. I thought you'd be interested," she began.

"You never give up, do you? You're an incurable romantic."

"I guess I am. But I was really looking for information about that harp I found. I'm having it restrung, you know; it belongs in the First Drawing Room. Really, Edan, it will be a lovely addition and so in keeping with the period of the house. I hope you agree."

"If you say so. I can see how careful you are and how much energy you're putting into this project. So go right ahead." He shrugged and turned away. Now that it was September, the nights grew cool very quickly. Mrs. Bateman had lighted a small fire in the grate.

"Don't you want to hear what I found out?"

He glanced toward her with the brooding look he sometimes wore, and she wondered if she ought to bother. She could not seem to pass on her own enthusiasm to this sulky, often remote man.

"If you want to read something to me, then of course I want to know. Go ahead."

She read him the bit about the harp and also about the priest hole leading to a clump of cedars.

"Wouldn't it be exciting if we could find out where the tunnel ended? Do you think that's possible?" she asked.

He did not reply at first. She had the distinct feeling he had not even heard her.

"Oh, what's the use? If *you* don't care, why should I? You don't make it very appealing to do a good job here, Lord Deane," she said, reverting to his formal title, a thing she sometimes did when she was annoyed. "I might as well stop wasting all my time and energy on this house. Let some decorator come in who doesn't care!"

He was instantly contrite.

"Maggie, I'm sorry."

He crossed the room swiftly and placed a hand on her shoulder. She felt the thrill of his touch, as she had so often in the past. The days and nights of staying away from him, of keeping to herself, had not destroyed the feeling she had for him. She forced herself to step back.

"Don't be sorry. I shouldn't expect you to feel this way. You have so many other interests. Things much more important than history."

"Would you like to take a walk before dinner? And explore the place where the tunnel might come out?"

She was eager to do so, but she made herself speak with reserve. "Yes, if we have time."

"Of course, we have time. I'd like a stroll anyway. We'll go and look for Rex, and give him a run."

Rex was the pup Mr. Farraday had favored in his litter. He had presented the dog to Edan when it was old enough to be separated from its mother. Most of Rex's time was spent around the stables, but he liked to romp with Edan when he was given the chance.

With the dog chasing behind, they made a long and rambling tour of the grounds close to the house. In the distance, near the lake, they could see that the folly roof had been repaired and freshly painted. Closer to hand, a new garden was being dug, ready for stone paths to be laid before the winter set in.

"Lady Amalie's journal mentioned that the end of the tunnel came out in a grove of cedars," Maggie ventured. "Do you suppose any one of these trees is old enough to be original?"

"I doubt it. My father ordered most of this planting done when I was still a child. I remember visiting here while he supervised it. However, we can make an educated guess about the tunnel. It would be in the straightest possible line from the house. They'd want to dig it in the easiest way possible. Let's see if we can find a spot here that's in direct line."

They selected the most likely position and examined the earth under the cedars, kicking aside layers of dirt, leaves that had blown across from the great oaks and pine needles from some trees nearby. They found no trace of a tunnel. Maggie felt let down. Seeing her dejection, Edan said, "Never mind, we won't give up yet. We'll have plenty of time to explore around here."

"Oh, dear," Maggie said, sighing, "I felt I was doing so well with my detective work. Anyway, the harp was a real find. I know it will add to the mood of the room."

"You're incorrigible." Edan laughed.

She thought she detected a touch of indulgence in his voice. Could he really be human at times? Once in a while in the past she had thought so, and then there were the other times—when he was cold, and impatient, and far too presumptuous.

After dinner, they sat reading together in the rent room. The fire crackled pleasantly. There was a comfortable air about the place, and when they climbed the stairs together at bedtime, Edan made no advances. He offered her a polite goodnight on the landing. She turned into her room alone, according to the rules, and that was what she wanted. That was all she had asked for when she came here, Maggie told herself. Respect for her work. Dignity. Time to do her job properly.

Then why did she feel so sad? So lost? So terribly alone?

Chapter Seven

September settled in. The chilly air, falling yellow-brown leaves, and uncertain gusts of wind made swimming impossible. The lake lay quiet at the bottom of the garden, no more than a mirror for a clouded sky or the focal point for a stroll. Maggie continued her riding lessons with Quinn, and sometimes she still took a sauna but she never again crossed paths with Edan in the little hut.

Days were filled with revised plans, shopping for materials in London, and supervising workmen. Maggie and Edan discussed some of her future schemes for the house, or his problems relating to the land or the tenants. They often shared a meal but the mood was different now: a kind of standoff. They held polite conversations with no emotional involvement or physical contact.

There were plumbers all over the house during the day. The chief worry now was not providing hot water for workable bathrooms, but the entire central heating system. Could the men possibly have it ready before cold weather set in? Fireplaces were charming and attractive, but they failed to heat a house properly. And Edan had made it quite clear that he was an Englishman who liked warm rooms. He was as anxious as Maggie to have the furnace in running order before the temperature dropped.

Almost every morning, when Maggie went riding with Quinn, Rex came along. The dog was almost as attached to her these days as he was to Edan and Quinn. He had won his way into the house more and more, overseeing the workmen and suggesting by his eager watchfulness that he was in charge of security.

Brenda Hawke was still on the scene too. Often she would telephone to invite Edan to Chagford Hunt for dinner but she did not suggest—not even once—that Maggie come along. Nor did she offer to show Maggie the house. When she thought about it, Maggie felt put out that Edan himself didn't give her a chance to view Chagford, since he knew how much she longed to see it. It was a source of mild irritation to her that Edan followed along with Brenda's snobbish ways.

Chagford Hunt had been built originally by Henry the Eighth as a hunting lodge and was, as a consequence, very large. There were many tales about the guests who had slept there: visiting princes, matchmaking lords, and beautiful women. Edan had told Maggie that the pigskin wallcovering, installed when the house was constructed, was still intact in the library. Much of the panelling in the huge halls and reception rooms was original, as well, and the windows were mullioned and the ceilings high. A few alterations had been made over the years, but Chagford was now considered one of the genuine treasures of Tudor times and could no longer be radically changed in any way.

In mid-September, Brenda did one of her swooping acts, as Maggie secretly called them. She arrived one morning while Edan was still at breakfast, without telephoning ahead. Her voice rang out from the front hall, piercing the cool morning and penetrating right into the breakfast room.

"Edan? Edan, darling, where are you?"

She knows perfectly well where he is, Maggie thought crossly, she knows he always has breakfast at this time. But it gives her a chance to interrupt, and to show me she's still in control. Really, she's the most revolting woman I've ever met.

Edan did not appear to notice her reaction. He called out, "In here, Brenda. Come and join us for coffee. We're just having our daily meeting about the work in progress."

She made an entrance—Brenda never just came into a room—wearing one of her beautifully tailored riding habits, her dark hair pulled smoothly back under the neat hat so carefully placed at a proper angle. Removing her gloves ceremoniously, she beamed a luscious smile toward Lord Deane.

Edan rose and pulled out a chair for her. He rang the bell for Mrs. Bateman and ordered more coffee. Rex happened to be leaning against Maggie's chair, his eye firmly fixed on the toast and marmalade. They never gave him any but Rex never lost hope. At Brenda's entrance, he gave a low growl.

Brenda flashed the dog an angry look.

"Really, Edan, that's a stupid animal! I don't know why you keep him. Why don't you get a dog with a pedigree, if you want one at all? From a proper kennel instead of from that silly old man down at the cottage. Why do you let him in the house? Dogs belong in kennels or stables. You know that perfectly well."

"My father always had one or two dogs around the house," Edan said lightly. "I rather like Rex."

"I *know* dogs," Brenda went on relentlessly. "We

always kept a pack of hounds, until I gave them up last year—they cost so much and I didn't think it was worth it any longer. But no dog has ever growled at me. It just proves he's an imbecile."

They were interrupted by Mrs. Bateman, who came in with fresh coffee and a cup for Brenda. Maggie had expected the conversation about the dog to die natural-ly, but Edan gave Brenda a stern look and said calmly, "Rex is intelligent. He's a friendly dog, too. I like him. He can come in here whenever he likes, as long as Mrs. Bateman doesn't complain."

"He's not friendly to *me*," Brenda said darkly. "You're too lenient with the help anyway, Edan. That's no way to run a place like Deane Park."

Poor Rex, if *she* ever becomes Lady Deane, Maggie thought. She'll either banish him to the stables forever, or have him put down at the vet's. As soon as the thought had come into her mind, Maggie felt guilty. She was always a trifle shocked by her reaction to Brenda. Usually, she got along extremely well with women.

"If you don't push these workmen, Edan," Brenda began again, "you'll have no heat in this place when the cold weather comes. Of course, they know you're easygoing and they take advantage. You must keep after them day after day, or they just slack off. But if you have such an inexperienced person in charge"— and here she looked at Maggie in a cool, appraising way—"naturally, you can't expect tradesmen to respect her. But you never listen, Edan. You never learn from others."

"Oh, now that's where you're wrong," Edan said lightly. "I can see quite clearly how you run Chagford, Brenda. And I *do* learn."

Was there just a touch of sarcasm there? Or was she imagining it, Maggie wondered.

"I've come to invite you to my costume ball," Brenda said next, ignoring Maggie. "At the end of October. Really, it's a party for the people who worked for us in the last by-election, but I decided to make it a gala. Everyone will be asked to dress as a historical figure."

"Sounds like fun, Brenda," Edan said. "I'll think of something."

"No need to think hard, darling. Since Chagford Hunt was built for Henry the Eighth, I thought I'd be Anne Boleyn. You could come as Henry. Think what a sensation we'd make!"

"I don't think I have the weight for it," Edan said, with little enthusiasm. "And Henry isn't my favorite character."

"Now, don't fuss, Edan. Think of the effect! I need you as *host,* darling, so it would look well if we're a couple. I couldn't give a party like this if I didn't have you as host."

Brenda smiled. When she put some effort into it, Maggie reflected, she could be quite beautiful. The whole party had probably been planned just so Edan would have to partner her. It was a nasty thought, but somehow Brenda always had this unpleasant effect upon her.

"I'll think about the costume," Edan agreed.

He obviously didn't like being told what to do, Maggie decided. Perhaps Brenda had gone too far.

"How about inviting Peter Cross?" Edan said brightly. "Maggie will need an escort. He can stay here with us for the weekend."

Brenda looked momentarily startled. As if she hadn't considered inviting Maggie and the idea of an extra escort was totally new.

"If you think so, it's a good idea," Brenda said sweetly. "I liked Peter, what I saw of him. Yes, why don't you do that? I believe you and Peter are a couple?" she said, addressing the question directly to Maggie.

"He's my employer. And we're friends, that's all."

"How nice. It takes the suspicion of fortune hunter off the whole enterprise then, doesn't it?"

"Brenda, that remark wasn't called for. I think you owe Miss Jordan an apology," Edan said.

"Did I say something wrong? I'm terribly sorry."

"Maggie, will you call Peter, then?" Edan said, trying to put the conversation back on a more friendly basis. "We ought to have him look over the work soon, anyway."

"I'll call him today. I want his opinion on some ideas, and when I spoke to him last week he said he was almost finished at Elwyn House. He'll be working in London on a couple of jobs, but for a special event I'm sure he'll be delighted to drive out. And I look forward to seeing your house, too, Miss Hawke."

"Really? I had no idea you took your work so seriously," Brenda said, rising. "I must run along, darling. Will you come to the party early? I'd like you to receive guests with me."

"Any time you say, Brenda. Your wishes are my command," Edan said, making a mock bow. "But wait a minute. Don't go yet. We're about to unveil the first room. I haven't been allowed in it for two weeks. Maggie is just about to open it up. Right after breakfast, in fact."

"You mean we are actually about to see the result of Miss Jordan's efforts?"

"Yes, the library," Edan said, waiting for Maggie and Brenda to precede him out of the room. "My special retreat. That's the room she's done first."

Maggie felt a bit like a performer on opening night. But she was proud of what she had done with the library. She had turned it from a drab, though comfortable room, into a bright, welcoming, but still restful place. She had begun with the chintz, a vibrant print of birds and flowers in vermilion and green on a black ground. The sofas and lounge chairs and the curtains were all done in the same material. A pair of armchairs —the ones she had selected from the attic— had been covered in vermilion velvet, with touches of gilt. And while the walls were light in color, the carpet was a rich brown. She had hung the portrait of an early Lady Deane—whom she liked to think was Amalie—over the fireplace. The whole effect was cheerful. A happy room.

She opened the door, and they stepped in. She glanced first at Edan and thought she detected the beginning of a frown. And then Brenda exclaimed:

"Oh, my dear. How awful! It simply isn't this house at all! I don't know how you could have done that! Surely you aren't going to turn the whole place into an advertisement for a draper's shop?"

Maggie turned cold. She saw Edan's face close up. Was he remembering all his old fears about a young, inexperienced woman restoring Deane Park?

"I'm not doing any of the other rooms in these strong colors," Maggie said defensively. "Only this one. I wanted it to be warm, a comfortable place to read, or listen to music, or work."

"Oh dear," Brenda said, backing away as if she had somehow stumbled into a pesthouse. "I mean, really, Edan darling, this house is so, well, *delicate*. So unlike Chagford, of course. But that doesn't mean I don't understand it. Because I do."

And *I* understand it, too, Maggie thought furiously. Why had she shown the library first? Before any of the other rooms were ready? The others would be in perfect harmony with the mood of the house.

"The colors are cheerful, certainly, but this isn't a restoration. It's out of character," Edan pronounced.

"So wrong!" Brenda cried, seeing Edan's displeasure. "I don't think you can afford to have one single room that's out of key. Like a wrong note in a symphony. That's how I feel."

Maggie wanted to ask who on earth cared how *Brenda* felt? But she didn't dare. She was on very thin ice now, she could see. If Edan lost faith in her, she wouldn't be able to complete the assignment. She had made a terrible error in letting him see the library before the First Drawing Room.

"The drawing room will be finished soon," Maggie said hastily. "And it's exactly in keeping with the house. Couldn't we wait until then for a judgment?"

"By then, it will be too late," Brenda said. "Frankly, darling, I wouldn't want to sit in here, it's too bizarre."

Edan said firmly, "Call Peter right away. We'll have him drive out and let him decide what's to be done. You can tell him then about your other plans, Maggie, and we'll see."

So she was on probation again. She ought to walk out on the lot of them right now, Maggie thought angrily. They were treating her as if she were a child.

"Yes, send for Peter Cross right away," Brenda agreed. "That's what I advise. Well, Edan, I must be off. Are you coming over for dinner tonight? You'll need consolation after this little disaster."

She sailed out of the room, leaving Maggie with the shreds of her creation, like the aftermath of a party that didn't quite work. The only cheering thing about the morning, so far, was the fact that Rex chased after Brenda, barking and growling, and was only brought under control when Maggie spoke to him. She had that much satisfaction, at least.

Edan did not appear for dinner. Maggie assumed from this that he had taken Brenda up on her invitation, following her like some inexperienced schoolboy. She was still in the library poring over paint samples and fabrics when she heard Edan come in.

"Enjoying the atmosphere?" Edan asked politely, pouring himself a whisky from the tray.

"Yes, I am, thank you," she said coolly. "I find I can work very well in this room. Actually, I told Bateman we won't be using the rent room anymore until it's redecorated."

"Did you call Peter?"

"Not yet. He's still at dinner, I imagine."

"He'll be back having a nightcap by this time. How about putting in the call right now?"

"You really believe I can't handle this assignment, don't you?" she asked icily, trying to conceal her hurt feelings. "Why don't you have faith in me until you've seen the First Drawing Room? I've tried to explain why I designed this room differently. I felt it would make a comfortable spot for you—a casual place. Some of the rooms are bound to be very formal. I don't think you'll like that over a long period of time."

"That makes sense, all right, but I'd feel better if you brought Peter into it right away. Don't you want to see him?"

"Naturally, I'd like to see him, but not when he's just undertaken a job in London. It isn't fair to drag him out here—to distract him now."

"You don't sound very anxious. Don't *you* think your work is good?"

"Yes, Lord Deane, I think my work is very good. However, I function quite independently. I have my own career, my own future to think of. I have to be able to manage on my own, not shout for help every time I find myself in difficulties. Not like *some* women."

"What's that supposed to mean?"

"Miss Hawke made a very rude remark to me.

Calling me a fortune hunter. She ought to have apologized properly and you ought to have forced her to do so. If you were a gentleman, as you claim."

"But you don't need any help. You just told me so."

"Oh, don't be difficult. I'll call Peter."

There was, at the moment, only one telephone in Deane Park. It was another of the changes that would be made. Eventually, there would be telephones in the library and the rent room, as well as the front hall. But for the moment she had no choice but to make the call from the drafty foyer.

Peter had just arrived in his flat and seemed pleased to hear from her.

"Have you begun the new job yet?" she asked.

"Yesterday. Mrs. Fitzsimmons—you remember her, don't you?—is already making waves. She has a flat in Eaton Mews and wants it turned into a palace. I tried to point out there isn't space enough for a palace, but she expects miracles. How are things going at Deane Park?"

"I'm having a bit of trouble, Peter, that's why I called." She wanted to get his attention without alarming him. "Not serious, but I know Edan would be happier if you came down soon. We were going to wait until October when Brenda Hawke is having a costume party at Chagford. But now he wants you to come immediately."

"I see. Well, I could drive out for a day or so, but not long. The new Dragon Lady is very demanding. But aren't they all? It's meeting after meeting and change after change. It's enough to make one dizzy. But she's willing to pay and that's the main thing, I guess. Let me look at my book."

There was a pause while he consulted his daybook, apparently, and then he was back on the line.

"Day after tomorrow. That's the soonest I can make

it. I'll stay overnight, and that will give us more time.
I'll look forward to seeing your lovely face after the
Dragon Lady's ferocity."

Peter arrived two days later in time for a drink before
dinner. It was one of those mellow autumn days when
the light is clear and the air smells like winey apples.
Maggie had looked forward to seeing him. It would be
nice to have some real support—nice to have some
compliments for a change instead of these eternal
scraps, these constant put-downs. She chose a woollen
dress the color of faded roses that made her look
terribly young, terribly vulnerable. She wanted Peter to
agree with her, to fuss over her, to show Edan Deane
that she had a true admirer, not only of her work, but
of her beauty.

It seemed that Peter, too, had missed her. He was
definitely in a mood to flatter and pamper.

"This country air agrees with you!" he said enthusiastically, as soon as she joined him in the library. "How
will we ever drag you back to London?"

"Do you think so?" She felt better already. "What is
your opinion of this room, Peter? That's what's bother-
ing Edan. As I'm sure he told you. I don't plan to do
the rest of the house like this. This room was meant to
be different. But Brenda Hawke doesn't like it, so Edan
doesn't like it."

Peter gave Edan a sharp look. "What does it have to
do with Brenda?"

"Nothing, except that she knows this house and so, I
value her opinion."

"Are you planning on bringing Brenda here as
mistress?" Peter asked directly.

Maggie waited breathlessly for the answer. She had
wanted to ask this very question herself but didn't dare.

"No, I haven't given that any serious thought," Edan
replied.

"Then I don't think we ought to consider Brenda's feelings," Peter said quickly. "I agree with you, Edan, that this style is not exactly in keeping with the rest of the house. But I think you ought to wait until Maggie has finished the First Drawing Room."

"That will be a bit late, won't it? All the money spent will be wasted if it doesn't work. I just don't know."

"She meant this room as a retreat for you. Do you like it? Do you find it cosy?"

"Very pleasant. Very comfortable."

"Then the room is a success."

"Now just a minute, Peter, we have to think of the overall restoration. *This* isn't a restoration—it isn't any period at all. It's a mish-mash."

"Have I time for one more whisky before dinner?" Peter asked, holding out his glass. "I know how punctual you are, Edan."

"Certainly. Let me get it for you."

"If you just hold your decision until the drawing room is ready," Peter went on. "I know what Maggie plans to do. I talked to her. She's keeping that wallpaper, and the colors will be muted. She found a wonderful carpet in storage, and when it's delivered, it will make all the difference."

"And the harp. Lady Amalie's harp," Maggie added.

"Her ideas for that room are very sound, Edan. Don't panic now, when things are going well."

Edan gave Maggie a harsh look but it softened suddenly.

"I'll do as you say, Peter," he said, and then with the old wicked grin, "and meanwhile, we'll use this mish-mash and try to enjoy it."

They discussed the heating system, the bathrooms, and the idea of the rent room as a small sitting room. Peter offered his advice and some new ideas quite freely. By the time they had reached coffee, Edan was more relaxed.

"It's settled, then," he said at bedtime. "I'll go along with Maggie's plan. I'll keep out of her way until I see the First Drawing Room. That's fair, isn't it?"

"That's all we ask," Peter said.

"I've got to go out to the stables," Edan said as they were about to say goodnight. "You two go along. I have to see Quinn about one of the horses."

Maggie watched him leave with a strange reluctance. Yet that was silly, she told herself. Peter was here with her and she hadn't seen him for a long time. He offered her a brandy and she accepted, although brandy was not something she cared much for as a rule.

"Yes, I'll have a nightcap with you," she said.

She hoped that Peter would sweep her into his arms, that he would woo her, convince her that she was beautiful and that they loved one another. That's what she wanted. The stability of Peter's affection, his appreciation for her career, his totally unchauvinistic view of life.

When they went upstairs, Edan had not come back. At her bedroom door, Peter said, "Let me come in, please. Just for a few moments, Maggie."

"Yes, all right."

And here it was. Her wish. The thing she had hoped would happen, *did* happen. Peter put his arms around her and drew her to him, easily and smoothly. His mouth came down on hers in a soft, affectionate kiss. She felt the familiar hands upon her shoulders, hands that were warm and tender. She recognized the cologne he wore. And yet, she failed to respond. She had wanted Peter to make love to her and everything had come about just as she had visualized it. Why then did she not feel gloriously happy?

She thought of Edan and the picture of him, the memory of the burning kisses he had forced upon her, the way his eyes had examined her that day in the sauna so that her blood coursed through her veins and her heart pounded, the way he had touched her when they were swimming, so that her skin felt blazing hot even in the cool water, the way he had weighed down upon her in such a sweetly painful way that night on her own bed in this very room! All of it flooded her mind. And she could not feel anything now when Peter kissed her.

It was no use. She pulled away.

"Please go, Peter. I'm tired. It was wrong of me to let you come in here."

"I thought you wanted to see me." He sounded hurt.

"I did. I do. Oh, I don't know!"

"It's Edan, isn't it? Women always fall in love with Edan."

"No, it isn't Edan," she lied. "I'm sure he's going to marry Brenda."

"You're in love with him."

"No, no, I'm not. I'm just disappointed in his reaction to the library, that's all. I really felt I'd done something worthwhile there. Oh, Peter, I don't know . . ."

"It won't do you any good to fall in love with Edan Deane. I told you that in the beginning."

He went to the bedroom door and opened it.

"Good night, Maggie," he said, pausing to look at her.

She felt sorry that she had encouraged him, and at the same time awkward. She stretched out her hand to him, to touch his arm, to convey that feeling of regret to him. A gesture that was only a means of making up.

And as she did so, she glanced past Peter's shoulder and there was Edan Deane staring at them, his face dark with some emotion she could not quite define.

"It's my turn to apologize," Edan said coldly. "Once, I recall, it was you, Peter, who came upon Miss

Jordan and me in the moonlight. And now I find the
roles reversed. Well, Miss Jordan is indeed a busy
person. Good night."

She wanted to call after him, to try to explain what
had happened. But as soon as she tried to form the
words, she knew it would sound childish, and that it
might not even ring true. For how could she explain
inviting Peter into her room in the first place?

As she closed the door on both of them, her heart
felt heavy, as if she had suddenly developed a terrible
problem that could not be solved. Perhaps that was
exactly the case, she told herself, for every attempt to
understand Edan Deane was hopeless, apparently.
And no matter how she behaved, it never seemed to be
right.

Breakfast next morning was strained, but somehow
they managed to get through it. Both Edan and Maggie
went out to the car with Peter to see him off.

"You *will* come to the costume party, won't you?"
Maggie asked a bit forlornly.

"If you want me to, certainly."

"Yes, we do want you to come," Edan assured him.
"You can stay here a couple of days if you have time,
Peter. We can combine the party with another meeting
about the house. The drawing room ought to be done
by then, wouldn't you say, Maggie?"

He was being friendly again, calling her by her first
name. It was his habit to switch back and forth to
indicate his pleasure or his displeasure. But the friendli-
ness was just on the surface, Maggie was sure.

"I'm sorry we don't agree on the library," Maggie
said wistfully as Peter's car disappeared over the hill.

"We agree on some things, at least. On keeping Rex
around the house, for example," he said.

"But not on the library chintz." She managed a
smile.

"Perhaps I'll get used to it and be absolutely wild

about the color scheme. Certainly I like the idea of hanging Lady Deane's portrait over the fire. Those little touches are fine, so we agree there."

"Then I'm being kept on, am I? You're going to let me finish the drawing room?" She could not quite keep the edge out of her voice.

"You have been saved from the villain, at least for the time being. Your hero rode to your rescue. It's just like a fairy tale, isn't it? Except I don't like the casting, not when I'm the villain."

"I've never thought of you as a villain, exactly."

"Good! Because I have another piece of news for you. The plumbers are having a devil of a time. There's only one bathroom working on the second floor from this morning on. It's the one down the hall, between our rooms. Yours will be cut off, I'm afraid. And so will mine. I hope you don't mind too much, but they say it might be two days. I told the foreman we couldn't possibly put up with one bathroom for any longer."

"It is a bit awkward, isn't it?"

That was putting the case mildly. If he wanted to be difficult, this would be a nice opportunity. Except that, lately, he had been behaving very correctly so she ought not to look for trouble.

"Even with your little disappointment, do you still feel as strongly about your career, Maggie Jordan?" he asked as they went back into the house together.

"I'm as serious as ever. I wouldn't give it up for anything. Do you know what my goal is? I want to be the best interior designer in all of England. Perhaps even internationally. I'm young, I have plenty of time to learn."

"I see. I thought you might have changed your mind about the importance of this kind of thing."

"Why would I?"

"No reason, I suppose. I just have some kind of built-in objection to women having serious careers. I guess I'm a leftover from the Victorian era—a dinosaur, out of fashion."

She immediately wanted to leap to his defence.

"I'm sure that's not true! Restoring a house like this is a big task. You're just under a bit of strain, that's all."

"Even *my* bank account may begin to crumble, if these plumbers don't finish the job soon," he said, sighing. "I had no idea there was so much to do. That it would take so long."

"Then why not agree, right away, to restore only certain rooms? You could leave the rest of the house until later. Perhaps, when you marry, your wife would like to make some of the decisions. For instance, Brenda has definite ideas about décor. You might want to consider her opinion."

"Brenda has her own house. I can't imagine her living anywhere but Chagford Hunt. You don't know that girl. A will of iron. I only listened to her ideas about Deane Park because she's known this house all her life. But I don't intend to decorate the house to Brenda's taste."

"She seems more interested in Deane Park than Chagford Hunt," Maggie pointed out. "I don't hear any plans for restoring *it*."

"No, no, Deane Park would seem small to her. That place she owns is huge."

"But she'd also have you," Maggie pointed out sweetly. "And that would make up for a dozen rooms, I should think."

He grinned.

"When you put it like that, yes. Having me would make this place extremely attractive."

"Nobody can say you're shy," Maggie muttered.

She saw little of Edan during that day. Her own work on the First Drawing Room was going ahead reasonably well, and by dinnertime she was ready to relax

with a book. Edan did not appear. She did not see him
at bedtime either, and decided to use the only working
bathroom while it was free. If either of them was to
have the benefit of hot water, it might as well be
Maggie.

She moved her toiletries and her supply of towels
into the bathroom down the hall. Then she undressed
in her bedroom and, wearing a pale-blue velour housecoat, went back for a relaxing bath.

She soaked in the tub, and then stepped out to dry
herself in the huge white bath sheet. She stood before
the full-length mirror that took up part of one wall—
like all the bathrooms in Deane Park it was a huge
room—and observed herself. She was reasonably attractive, she decided modestly. Men had used more
extravagant phrases than that, of course. She wondered
if they were right.

Her mother had come from a Swedish background
and so she was a real blonde. No hair dye for her,
fortunately. Her skin was naturally pale but tanned
easily. From summer bathing, she had acquired a light
tan everywhere except the areas covered by the skimpy
bikini she had bought especially for sunbathing. She
had pinned up the honey-colored hair and it gave her a
statuesque look. Yes, she did have nice firm breasts,
and a small waist. And slim hips, too, molded into
smooth, long legs.

Why then did Edan prefer Brenda? Because she was
brought up to his way of life. And because she didn't
want a career but would be content to stay home and
look after Deane Park, as he felt it should be looked
after. And Edan, as well.

It was useless to ask these questions when she knew
the answers. Totally useless to care about a man like
Edan Deane. Yet she continued to stare at her naked
body and to dream of a man she could not have! She
must have lost her senses.

She heard the door handle turn. And stood rigid, powerless to move. The reflection of herself stared back, and faced the door, too. He stood there, poised, hand still on the knob.

"Oh. I'm sorry. I thought the bathroom was empty. You didn't put the lock on."

"I forgot."

She had also forgotten to grab the towel because she felt so paralyzed at his appearance. It was several seconds before this thought occurred to her. And in that time a look of passion swept through Edan's dark eyes. He wore a robe that he had neglected to fasten.

Maggie almost fainted with desire and fear—a desire to have Edan take her in his arms, and a fear that she would surrender. Then he seemed to grow cold right before her eyes, and pulling the belt tightly around his robe, he spoke.

"You know, Miss Jordan, I do believe you're a tease. Better put that towel on before you drive me to distraction."

"You needn't have come in," she pointed out. "And you could leave right this minute, if you're so distracted."

She picked up a towel and draped it around herself. He backed out, still looking at her candidly, but without that first momentous flush of need. —

When he had gone, she felt like weeping. She was a fool. She always seemed to behave like a fool when Edan Deane was around. And she had never in her life wanted more desperately to behave in a sophisticated, intelligent way.

The real trouble was, she thought as she lay in bed, that for once in her life she did not know what she wanted. And she therefore did not know how to act. On the one hand, she adored the job here at Deane Park. She loved the house and its possibilities, and she recognized the prestige involved. It gave her satisfaction, too, to restore its beautiful rooms and to pursue the story of Lady Caroline and Lord Byron and to browse in Lady Amalie's journals.

On the other hand, she ought to leave. It was obvious that Edan Deane and she would never get along—not really. He was attracted to her but only in the most physical way, apparently. And she was drawn to him. But these encounters, which brought out the worst side of her nature, must stop. And how were they to stop if she kept on seeing Edan Deane?

Well, she resolved, she would stay at least until the First Drawing Room was complete. She must vindicate her judgment after the disagreement in the library. She must prove that she knew how the house should be decorated, that she had sensed its mood.

With this firmly in mind, she went to sleep. Only to dream of Edan Deane; a peculiar mixture of images in which, somehow, she had become Lady Amalie and he Lord Deane of those distant times and they were married and living here at Deane Park—and it was very, very lovely.

Chapter Eight

Throughout the rest of September, Maggie continued her riding lessons. Quinn had assumed more and more duties, supervising much of the outside work as well as caring for the horses. He and Edan together had hired extra help to prepare some of the unused gardens around the house for spring planting. Workmen still swarmed over the place, outside and in; installing the new heating system, the plumbing, painting walls and laying carpet. There was so much activity that Maggie found it quite easy to avoid Edan, especially during the day. She stayed much to herself. At meals, they used the time to discuss aspects of the restoration but they didn't touch on personal subjects.

By October, the days had grown even chillier and the great house creaked and whispered in the wind. The heating plant sprang to life at last and the rooms were warm. She and Edan used the library constantly, as a place to work and a place to read or listen to Edan's collection of records. It had become an island in the chaos that seemed to permeate the rest of the house. Her ideas continued to flourish, too, and she saw more and more interesting possibilities in the whole effect that might be created in Deane Park.

In the middle of the month she had a call from Everly Jones. Caroline Lamb had definitely painted the picture. Maggie was breathless with excitement when she announced the news to Edan.

"Don't you see? This proves she stayed here."

"*I'm* pleased if *you're* pleased," he said. "Although I don't know what difference it can possibly make to my life."

"It adds something to the house. To its history, that's all," she said, ignoring his lack of enthusiasm. "After all, you're a Byron fan, too. You know more of his poetry than I do."

They were in the library having a drink before dinner. A fire blazed merrily in the grate, casting a warm glow over Lady Amalie's features. Maggie had made up her mind that this Lady Deane *was* Amalie.

Mrs. Bateman came in and announced dinner. Bateman was busy in the wine cellar, she said apologetically, but would be up in time to serve at table.

" 'That all-softening, overpowering knell, The tocsin of the soul—the dinner bell,' " Edan said, quoting from Byron's *Don Juan*. "Shall we go?"

Not to be outdone, Maggie searched desperately in her mind for a quick reply. She must show him that she, too, knew her Byron. She came up with an appropriate quote from a later stanza in the same poem.

" 'All human history attests that happiness for man— the hungry sinner—since Eve ate apples, much depends on dinner.' "

"Very good! You always manage to outmatch me."

Maggie would have to decide where to hang the little painting when Everly Jones returned it from London. She had hoped to establish in which bedroom Lady

Caroline Lamb had slept. That would have been the perfect spot. But it was apparently quite impossible. Her mind had never relinquished the idea of restoring the rent room and turning it into an alternate sitting room. After all, it provided a totally different view from the library's, and it could be done in period and still be made comfortable. Perhaps it would be a good place for the special picture.

Two days before Brenda's costume party, Peter Cross arrived at Deane Park. And that same night, the First Drawing Room was ready for the unveiling. Maggie was nervous, for so much depended upon Edan's acceptance of her restoration in this particular room. The drawing room must rescue her from the uncertainty about the library décor and place her firmly in charge of all restoration of Deane Park. Or—and this she could not bear to contemplate—it would cause her to be sacked from the job.

"I think we ought to have one drink in the library first," Peter said, giving Maggie a friendly, blue-eyed look. "And then form a procession. Headed by Maggie the Magician, of course. She can fling open the doors and say *'Voilà!'* "

"A little elaborate, but apt," Edan agreed. "I've told Bateman to stand by with the Dom Perignon. If the room's a success, it's champagne all the way tonight."

"I'm terrified!" Maggie said, looking from one to the other. Her eyes were huge, and she felt her fingers tremble on the glass of sherry.

"So you should be!" Peter said, pretending to be pompous. "Such a responsibility for such a little girl."

"All right!" Maggie said suddenly, setting down her glass. "Let's do it now. Before the suspense turns me into a wreck."

They put down their glasses and, both men waving her on with courtly gestures, they walked across the hall to the drawing room. The double doors were closed. Maggie had already turned the lights on in the room, so there was nothing for it but to swing the doors open and march in.

And there it was. Gracious and glittering—from the gilded ceiling to the Chippendale-style mirrors, from the ormolu and gilt chairs to the antique wallpaper with gold flowers and leaves entwined. The enormous rose-beige carpet had had its color restored to an unexpected warmth. The sofas were pale-green and gold brocade, and the harp, completely refurbished, beckoned from the far side of the room. It was spectacular.

"Superb," Edan said, smiling at her. "Congratulations, Maggie Jordan! It's exactly the way it should be."

"Yes, you've done it. The harp is the final touch. But every single detail—the wallpaper cleaned up beautifully, didn't it?—everything is perfect. I couldn't add a thing."

"Champagne," Edan announced. "We'll drink a bottle right here in this room. To christen it. I'll ring for Bateman."

Maggie wanted to cry. She was both happy and relieved. A great weight had been lifted from her mind. This was her first real solo job, and although she had consulted Peter often, the ideas were her own. The theme, and most of the decisions, belonged to Maggie Jordan.

Dinner had the aura of success. All the stresses of earlier meetings vanished, until the question of the costume party arose.

"Who are you impersonating?" Peter asked Edan.

"Are we supposed to tell? I thought I'd surprise everyone. Isn't that half the fun?" Edan said. It was apparent that he did not intend to reveal his scheme.

"And you Maggie? What are you wearing?"

"It's a secret."

"That isn't fair," Peter protested. "How am I sup-

posed to dress when I don't know your plans? I thought
we were supposed to be a couple, too. Edan and
Brenda aren't the only pair in the scheme, you know."

"Why don't you guess?" she asked, perversely.

She had no idea why she was being so difficult.
Peter's idea was a good one: they ought to go as a
couple; they ought to discuss their costumes. It would
be much more successful that way. Especially since
Brenda had made it clear that she expected Tudor
clothes to match the house. And that she and Edan
were to be a twosome.

"Jane Seymour, I suppose," Peter said. "She was
rather a romantic figure, wasn't she? Well, I'll make my
plans in secret, too. I can rent something quite smashing in London."

This announcement did nothing to cheer her. True,
she was anxious to see Chagford. But the sight of
Brenda and Edan as a loving couple was not enchant-
ing. Try as she would, she could not rid herself of this
imaginary scene: the two of them greeting people,
smiling, Edan spending the whole evening lavishing
attention on Brenda. At dinner she drank rather more
champagne than was good for her, trying to forget.

Next evening when she arrived in the library dressed
for the drive to Chagford Hunt, she found Peter
dressed as a Tudor peer.

"How do I look? I sent specially to London for it. It
came in a cab." And then he stared at her, forgetting
his own fancy dress.

"I ought to have known! *Lady Caroline!* Why didn't I
guess? We are rather mismatched, aren't we? By about
two hundred years. Turn around and let me see how
you look."

She had pinned up her blond hair into a thick bun
that sat at the nape of her neck. The sides were pulled
gracefully over the ears, and little tendrils curled about

her cheeks. It was a soft, flattering hairdo and gave her
an old-world look. She had made a large picture hat
from two old straw garden bonnets she had found in the
attic, and after wrapping it about with pale pink
chiffon, she added a large silk rose. Her gown was
low-cut, in the Empire style, with a gauzy effect around
the bust. She wondered if she had gone too far, made it
too revealing, but she rationalized that she had only
copied pictures of the period. It hung straight from the
bust in soft folds right to the ankles. She was a vision in
pink and white.

"Stunning," Peter pronounced. "You'll be the belle
of the ball."

"What about Brenda? I'm sure she's planned her
costume ever since she thought of the party."

To impress Edan, she wanted to add. She was certain
that while Brenda had claimed the party was a reward
for political workers who had given free time, it was
just an excuse to show off to Edan Deane. To lure him,
if she could, into a proposal. And what if he did
propose? What then? Would Maggie still be invited to
carry on with the restoration at Deane Park? Not
likely. Brenda had made it quite clear from the beginning that she did not approve of Maggie's taste.

Perhaps he wouldn't propose. She recalled Edan's
words not so long ago—"Brenda has her own house. I
can't imagine her living anywhere but Chagford Hunt."
That's what he had said. But then, men were notably
scatterbrained when it came to the women they married. He hadn't even thought it through, more than
likely.

Edan had made the journey to Chagford much
earlier, following Brenda's instructions, so no one had
seen his costume. Trying to imagine him as Henry
the Eighth was impossible. He simply did not have the
ruddy look or the full, square figure, let alone the
paunch.

Maggie and Peter, an oddly disparate couple, drove to the party in his gray Mercedes. By the time they arrived, the driveway was half-filled with a mixture of cars, large and small, old and new.

"I see the yeoman are out in full force," Peter said, eyeing the motley collection. "They wouldn't miss a bash like this for anything. It's a wonder there isn't an ambulance and a couple of wheelchairs."

"You can't blame them. I want to see the house myself," Maggie said.

"Curiosity, of course, and a free chicken dinner. They want to goggle at the inner sanctum of the rich. I'll bet they use every bathroom in the place, just so they can peek at the appointments."

Chagford was impressive. A great pile of red brick with mullioned windows and turrets, balustrades and wings shooting off in every direction. Only the main wing was the original hunting lodge, and the remainder had been added at various times over the centuries.

They found Brenda and Edan receiving in the great hall, with its two-storey ceiling and rich panelling. Her dark hair was smoothed back, her bodice tight, her bosom sufficiently bare to be provocative, and her skirt a bell of satin covered with fake beads. She rustled with every move and looked every inch the winsome queen.

The appearance of Edan, receiving beside Brenda, came as something of a shock. There, instead of a hearty Henry in brocade and fur, stood a dark and dashing figure in bottle-green velvet, white ruffled shirt, and long, flowing tie. His thick black hair was appropriately shaggy, straying over his forehead in a boyish way, his eyes were mysterious, his mouth cynical. What a funny couple they made! Maggie wanted to laugh. For even at a distance she could sense Brenda's barely concealed fury.

Both couples were completely at odds. It gave a peculiar effect. The entire evening was like that, as far

as Maggie was concerned. Movements back and forth
in time. Most guests had chosen Tudor costumes—
either Brenda had suggested it along with the invita-
tions, or they had decided for themselves to fit sartori-
ally into the mood of Chagford Hunt. Now and then
some oddity would appear with a wine glass in hand—a
personage from a different age, which upset the time
sense. But throughout the evening, drifting through the
rooms, there was the wispy figure of Lady Caroline,
accompanied by a Tudor courtier in doublet and hose.
And an icy Anne Boleyn with a wild, and smiling,
Byron.

Whenever Maggie saw Edan and Brenda together,
she felt a pang of unease. Or was it jealousy? No, it
couldn't be that, because Edan had every right to be
with Brenda. They belonged together. Except they
didn't look as if they did. And why had he deliberately
flouted Brenda's wishes? He knew perfectly well she
wanted him to appear as the king to her queen. A last
bit of rebellion, perhaps, before Brenda finally seized
control. Was Edan aware of her real character?

Drinks were being served in the long gallery, and
Peter and Maggie walked there, sightseeing as they
went. Chagford Hunt was a vast and magnificent house,
but a bit shabby, as if nothing had been done for a long
time to keep up the woodwork or restore damaged
floors. At one end of the room, a trio played baroque
music: a sackbut—a sort of brass horn that was ances-
tor to the trombone—lyre, and flute. A nice touch,
Maggie thought, giving Brenda a mark for taste.

In the ballroom a contemporary orchestra played
dance music. A great many plants had been brought in
to make the place more attractive. Many of the larger
rooms in the house were cold, and there wasn't much
furniture. Brenda needed to refurbish her own house,
Maggie decided, never mind giving her opinions about
Deane Park.

"Would you like to dance?" Peter asked. "Or would you like to see the library. That's where the famous pigskin wallcovering is. I'm sure Brenda wouldn't mind, since it's part of our professional role to see these things."

"Is it really the original, do you think?"

"That's what they say. There aren't many walls like that left in England. There is one room lined in pigskin at Great Fosters, I believe, which is another of Henry's houses. But they're rare. Shall we take a look?"

After several wrong turns, they found the library. Because so many rooms had been added on, there was no logical plan to Chagford. And when they did find it, the library was not only empty, but quite chilly, despite the fire in the grate. The high ceilings made rooms hard to heat, which was why, Peter pointed out somewhat vaguely, the Tudors wore so many furs indoors.

The pigskin coverings, stretched between darkly stained wood panels, proved to be in good condition and quite attractive. Maggie had expected them to be ugly but the skin was smooth as silk and a lovely cocoa shade, with the familiar tiny indentations seen on pigskin gloves.

They took a seat before the fire.

"How long do you expect to be at Deane Park?" Peter asked, breaking a rather long silence.

"All winter, I guess."

"That long? I hadn't realized—"

"You wanted me to take the job. It was *your* idea. Naturally, if Edan wants to go ahead—and now that he's so enthusiastic about the drawing room, I assume he *will*—then it will be a long, long task to pull the house together. I've barely started on the other principal rooms. The dining room will be a big project. And I have an idea about turning the rent room into a sitting room. There are so many things to do. I haven't given much thought to the front hall—and the staircase—and the bathrooms—" She trailed off, lost in a mixture of thoughts.

"I know I wanted you to take the assignment. It seemed a good idea. But I failed to realize how long you'd be away from London."

"You haven't been in London much yourself, Peter."

"No, but I will be during the winter. I have two flats to do. One in Chelsea and one in Knightsbridge. Then the Marchioness wants me to take a look at a house she's considering. She hasn't actually bought it yet, she wants my advice. I wish you were back there—I miss you."

Maggie chose to ignore his final words. She was very fond of Peter, but she sensed his feelings went beyond mere fondness.

"Which Marchioness? How can you expect me to know if you just say 'the Marchioness'?"

"The Marchioness of Lymington-West. I thought I told you."

"No, you didn't."

He took her hand, "I do miss you Maggie. Will you consider giving up this job at Deane Park? And coming back to London? Edan can easily find someone else to do it, you know. He has all sorts of contacts." He squeezed her hand and moved closer.

She didn't want Peter to become so intimate. She had the terrible feeling he was about to propose.

"You know I can't do that," she said, moving away from him slightly. "I love Deane Park!"

"It's all this romantic nonsense about Lady Caroline and Byron!" he cried, exasperated. "The next thing I know you'll be telling me you're a reincarnation of her. Well, she was a bit crazy. I wouldn't dwell too much on Caroline, if I were you."

"Passionate. Not necessarily crazy."

"Look, Maggie, I wish you'd come back to London. I've decided it's time I got married. I've avoided marriage long enough, but a man ought to have an anchor, a family."

"But I'm not ready for a family. Not yet! What about my career? You said—"

"All right, all right. No children for a while. You can work forever, if you like. Only come back to London. Marry me, Maggie."

So there it was, out in the open at last—Peter had proposed. If she had never come to Deane Park, she might have eventually accepted. That was the frightening thing. She turned to look at Peter, at his blond good looks, his open, friendly face. The honesty which she felt he possessed was reflected there. Surely those things counted? What did it matter if he failed to excite her? The wild feelings she had when Edan Deane touched her were probably false. She was wicked to feel like that about a man she hardly knew. That was no way to decide one's future, to choose one's fate. And it would all wear off anyway. Besides, Edan was interested in Brenda, and she was a fool.

"Peter, I—I . . ." she said hesitatingly.

He pulled her gently to her feet and put his arms around her. She allowed herself to be drawn into the safety of his embrace. Into the comfort of his words, his mouth soft on her cheek, his body close, but not persuasive, against her own.

"Look, darling, you don't have to decide right this minute. Think it over. A few days. Find out what you want to do about Deane Park. Perhaps Edan will want to cancel the restoration anyway, and all this talk about returning to London will be meaningless."

"Yes, yes, I'll do that. I'll think it over."

She grasped at the straw of indecision. She knew she could never have Edan, but she didn't want to hurt

Peter by marrying him on the rebound. Peter didn't have one harsh bone in his body, nor one iota of desire to overpower her. Or any woman. He was fair. He was generous. He was sweet.

"Good. Let's go back and have another glass of Brenda's house wine."

As they passed the ballroom, the strains of a waltz floated out to meet them. Edan was lounging in the archway, watching the dancers. He detained Maggie as she passed, putting a hand on her arm.

"Lady Caroline! I've been looking everywhere for you. This is our waltz, I think."

She paused and her eyes caught his avid glare. He seemed determined to make fun of her.

"Lord Byron! I'm so sorry, but I'm busy."

"Ah, but surely your friend won't object? Sir, may I have permission to dance with your lady?" He swept a courtly bow to Peter, as if he held a hat in his hand.

"Go ahead, Maggie. Don't be foolish. Of course you can dance with this madman."

Edan took her hand and led her to the floor, where she soon discovered that he was an excellent dancer. But naturally, he *would* be. She followed him easily, but they had no sooner made one turn around the ballroom than he held her close and began to whisper in her ear.

"Maggie, Maggie. I've thought about this all night."

"Stop it, Edan. People are looking at us."

"Only because we look so good together. So right."

She had a feeling that was partly true. They did look good together; his dark good looks and her fair ones. Their costumes matched, they were a pair of lovers. And as she sailed about in his arms, she almost believed that they were lovers in real life, not just for the duration of this dance.

When the waltz ended, he swept her into a small

alcove behind a screen and began to kiss her passionately. She tried to thrust him away, but was unsuccessful until he had had his fill of kisses. Then, as she panted and gave him a furious look he said, "Tell me, Maggie, is that how Peter kisses you?"

"That's not your business."

"Ah, but it is. And I venture to guess, my lovely Maggie, that Peter is rather more restrained in his lovemaking."

"You're disgusting."

"You think so? Then I might as well have the game as the name, to quote somebody's old saw."

With this, he began to kiss her again, running his lips over her face, across her eyelids, down her neck, down over the fine bones of her bare shoulder, to where the pale curve of her breast was thrust upward by the underpinnings of the gauze bodice. She struggled against him, though this only seemed to make him madder with desire, forcing her to push against his chest with her fists. Then he shocked her into silence by pulling down the bodice of her gown so that she was almost as naked as that day in the sauna.

"Mmmmm. What a beautiful sight you are, Maggie."

"You're despicable."

"Your darling Lord Byron would have done exactly this. If he had been fortunate enough to find himself exposed to such loveliness. Do you think he would have waited for your permission? Waited for the right moment? It is always the right moment, Maggie. Always."

The old familiar weakness flooded through her veins—that insane mixture of love and urgency, of delight and anger. Momentarily, his arms were the only thing that kept her from collapsing. He covered her lips again with his own, sipping her sweetness. She returned the light kiss with a fire she hadn't known she possessed.

"Maggie, Maggie," he murmured.

A voice, somewhere farther along the gallery, but obviously coming nearer every second, broke the spell.

"Edan, Edan darling, where are you? It's time to go into the dining room and help the guests—"

"Straighten your hair, Lady Caroline," Edan whispered. "I think the queen is approaching. You do look a bit distraught."

"Well, it's *your* fault," she hissed, quickly hitching up her dress, rearranging the wisps of hair, and hoping that she didn't have lipstick blurred around her mouth.

"Now, now, you enjoyed it. You're just like *her*." And then he stepped out from behind the screen. "Here I am, Brenda, I was just showing Lady Caroline some of the fine points of the panelling."

It was peculiar. Brenda as Queen Anne, walking regally toward them, smiling. Beside her, a handsome courtier, dressed in clothes that complemented hers. They might have been visitors from an era almost four hundred years earlier—in this hunting lodge—while from behind them came the sound of the baroque trio. They were Peter and Brenda, who had just been on a tour of the house, he now explained.

"Brenda has kindly shown me all the highlights, and I must say this house is a treasure trove. It lacks only a few touches to make it perfect, to make it shine. But I'm going to see if I can talk Brenda into some restoration later on."

Although she and Peter looked like a perfectly matched couple, Brenda came directly toward Edan as soon as she saw him. Her smile was for him and she ignored Maggie entirely.

"Even though it's a buffet, I must be there to see that guests are well looked after," she explained. "Will you stand with me, Edan?"

She saw Edan shrug, but follow politely, and once more the couples switched. Time, which was getting such a shaking up tonight, was once more altered.

"You seem a bit flustered," Peter remarked to Maggie. "Does the house have such a powerful effect on you as all that?"

"And you seem terribly pleased. Found yourself another assignment? Brenda seems too stingy with her money to put herself in your hands, Peter. The whole place looks shabby."

"Ah, but what possibilities! I'd love to do it over."

"Shall we go to the dining room with the others? I'm famished."

She tried to put Edan's kisses out of her mind. Tried to think about Peter, about her own assignment, about other jobs she might do in London. But her heart was still beating too rapidly, and she felt warm, although many of the rooms were chilly.

Near the end of the evening, when she went upstairs to the bedrooms where all the wraps were laid upon beds, chairs, and sofas, she felt so exhausted. In some ways she had enjoyed the party, but in others she felt dissatisfied. Seeing Edan with Brenda was upsetting, even if he *had* defied her about his costume. What was that, after all, but the act of a small boy? A childish rebellion? If he'd really wanted to put Brenda in her place, he wouldn't have gone off with her to the dining room in that docile fashion. She put on her velvet wrap and picked up the straw hat. No point in putting it on now, she decided, she'd simply carry it to the car.

As she descended the stairs, she saw no sign of Peter. Perhaps he was in the library, examining the extraordinary wallcovering once more. She walked in that direction, searching for him. At the door she heard voices. A meeting with Brenda, perhaps, trying once more to persuade her to redesign Chagford.

"Will you, Edan? Please say you will."

Brenda's voice, coaxing and strangely soft. Breathy with her need to have what she wanted. Maggie, frozen in the doorway, had come too far to back away. She

saw them standing there, close together. Brenda was
looking up at him, her eyes wide, her hand on his arm
as if to draw him closer.

"I've wanted you for a long, long time. Everyone will
be so pleased, darling, I know they will. Please say you
will."

Edan had his back to Maggie and the door, looking
down on Brenda. Then, in that beautiful voice which
Maggie had come to love so much, which excited her
beyond any voice she had ever imagined, he said,
"Since you propose it, I believe I will."

And he laughed.

"Oh, Edan, that's wonderful. Darling, that's wonderful!"

Brenda reached up, and with her two slim hands
pulled his face down and kissed him. Maggie fled.

Peter was waiting for her in the great hall.

"Let's go." Maggie said. "I feel rather ill."

All the way home, she forced herself to be calm.
She forced herself not to show emotion, not to cry. She
excused her silence and her strangeness by saying she
felt unwell. "Perhaps it was the chicken," she added,
helplessly. "I thought I took too much. And I guess I
did."

Peter was kind, as always. He didn't argue. How
could he know that, in reality, she was not physically
sick? That her soul was crushed? He would hear the
news soon enough, doubtless. And then he might
guess. But until that time, she only wanted to get to her
room. To be alone. To hide.

Brenda had proposed. That was the truth of it. And
Edan had accepted. Not with too much vivacity, but
still she had actually heard him accept. So there was no
use trying to fool herself about it. She had heard Edan's
words. The two of them had been so absorbed in what
they were saying that they had not even noticed her.

Brenda had won. Well, let them live in Deane Park,

or Chagford Hunt or anywhere else, what did she care? Somehow she stumbled up the stairs to her room, somehow she said goodnight to Peter, without actually crying. Somehow she prepared for bed and got into it, but she did not sleep.

She could not even bear the thought of telling Peter she was leaving. As soon as it was morning, she would pack, get in her car, and drive back to the city, but she would not speak to Peter nor would she speak to Edan. She couldn't go through the hypocrisy of congratulating him on his coming marriage. That would be too painful.

When it was light, Maggie got up, put on a warm pair of trousers and a bulky sweater, and began to pack. She wrote a note for Peter and shoved it under his door on the way downstairs. She would call him at the office the following day, she said, but felt like staying in her flat to recover from a kind of flu. He would find out soon enough why she had left Deane Park and the assignment. That announcement, she said, would come from Edan. No use waiting to be fired by Brenda, she told herself, when a slight doubt crossed her mind about her behavior. It might look like cowardice, but it was really practical.

Deane Park would belong to Brenda and, since she had made it clear from the beginning that she disapproved of Maggie's taste, why wait to hear the news?

As she carried her bags to the garage and put them in the car, she decided that she must say goodbye to Quinn, and to Rex as well. She would miss the dog. They had become fond of one another. And Quinn, for some reason, had become almost a friend. She had always cheered for him, right from the beginning, and had been delighted when she was proved right. Quinn had taught her a great deal about riding, too, and she had become much better in a short time than she could have hoped. She would miss the morning rides.

As she reached the stables, Quinn was just coming

out into the cold October morning, with Rex beside him.

"Good morning, Quinn."

"You're not dressed for riding," he observed.

"No, I've come to say goodbye. I'm leaving."

Rex seemed to know what she was saying. He rushed to her and she gave him a hug.

Though Quinn was not a man to show much emotion, she could see that he was surprised.

"Leaving? I thought you were here for the winter."

"So did I. I can't tell you why, because it's really news that should come from Lord Deane. He'll explain."

"I see."

He looked as if he already knew. Quinn was observant. He must have seen how Brenda Hawke behaved when she visited Deane Park. How possessive she was.

"Something to do with Miss Hawke?" he asked, as he walked with her toward the garage.

"Something like that," she said, still afraid she was going to break down when it came to saying goodbye to Rex. "I hope—I hope they don't decide to get rid of Rex. Miss Hawke doesn't like him."

Rex wanted to get in the car. She prevented him.

"So that's the way it is," Quinn said, knowingly.

She climbed in the car and Quinn opened the doors for her to back out.

"Look after Rex for me, Quinn," she said, and waved as she turned the corner of the buildings. There was a mist over the house, softening the lines. Just as there had been that first day. The day she had come to Deane Park as a stranger. How could she have known then how much she would come to care for the place? She passed the two stone lions. They looked mournful in the cool October morning.

She made the journey in a daze. Later, thinking it over, she could not recall how she had negotiated the traffic. Her flat, which had once seemed so large, so elegant, was now cramped. The bay window, which she had so admired, looked tiny after the great windows at Deane Park, and the small-scale furniture, even the Japanese screen she had considered such a prize, all suddenly looked like the objects in a dollhouse.

When Peter returned, she would meet him to discuss another assignment. If he had two houses to do in London, there would be work for her. Details were time-consuming and he would probably be pleased to have her help. Also, if he was serious about his marriage proposal, he would be delighted to have her company at dinner most evenings.

Yes, once she immersed herself in work, life would go on just as it had before. She had lived comfortably before she met Edan Deane and she could live happily once more. Time was the essential factor.

That night, the telephone rang, and she leaped to answer it. But, of course, it was Peter. He expressed surprise at her abrupt departure.

"Edan is confused. He wants to know why you did this. Why you didn't discuss it."

"He *knows* why, Peter. He's just pretending. Anyway, that's between him and me. Let's just accept the fact that I'm finished at Deane Park. You have other work I can do, haven't you?"

"Of course. Too much work. In fact, I plan to be away from London for a few days. I *am* glad to have you back, Maggie, it's just that I don't like leaving business arrangements up in the air like that."

"Don't worry about it. Edan knows why I left. He's just trying to make you feel bad about it."

"Still, I'd feel better if you at least called Edan."

She knew that she could not do that. That she would never give in to that extent, never let him know how much she had wanted to stay on, to be near him. And how much she disliked Brenda Hawke.

"Edan will tell you all about it one of these days," Maggie said with a heavy sigh. "Then you'll understand. I'll come in to the office tomorrow and we can discuss just what assignment you wish to give me."

"I've a small restaurant to do, in Mayfair. They want something very stylish, low-key, elegant. That might be perfect for you. I know you haven't done a restaurant, but you can assess the ones that are most popular at the moment and find out what makes them work. Then do your own version. How's that?"

"Oh, that's perfect. I knew you'd come through."

Peter was wonderful, not lecturing, not putting her through an inquisition, as some men would have done. And then quickly coming up with the answer—a job to distract her. She ought to fall in love with him. If she had a grain of common sense, that's what she would do. And together, they could build up the most fantastic business.

In the next two weeks, she spent all her time visiting restaurants, not just to dine or lunch, but with an eye to what made them popular, what people liked. And the practical side, too.

Often she was accompanied by Peter, and they discussed the décor together, but at other times she went alone. She struggled to keep her mind on this new problem, but sometimes, in the middle of a design for a public eating place, she thought of the dining room at Deane Park. She hadn't started on that room, not really. And there was so much to do! Such unusual ideas came to her. She thrust them aside. The restaurant. She must think of a chic theme, something different, something that would lure the fashionable trade. That was where her future lay now, not back at Deane Park.

Chapter Nine

The days of November stretched endlessly ahead. Maggie tried to bury herself in work. But even the restaurant was a link with Deane Park. Searching for a theme, she had hit upon the notion of designing it as a summer house—an interpretation of the folly on Edan's estate. And in the end the owner decided to call the place The Folly. It was done with pale-green latticework walls, an overhead skylight, and vines, with cream-colored woodwork. As she worked on it and saw it come to life, memories of the folly which she had loved so much, and which was now lost to her, made the experience both painful and exciting.

There would be an opening party for friends and an exclusive list of potential clients and media people. Maggie, along with the owner and the chef, would be one of the stars.

It should have been exciting. After all, Peter and the owner, too, had given her free rein with the design of the restaurant. It was the first big job she had done completely on her own, and there would be an audience when the doors were thrown open.

On the surface, she tried to appear happy. Yet in quiet moments, alone with her drawings, walking from shop to shop, at night in her elegant flat, she found her mind inevitably drifting back to Edan and the rolling lands of Deane Park. She wondered how Quinn was, and if he had managed to keep Rex. What if Brenda decided to get rid of the dog? When this thought occurred, she would push it away because she could not bear to think of Rex being given away, or destroyed.

She saw Peter sporadically: for dinner, at the theatre, or in meetings to discuss her restaurant project. Peter frequently went out of town, since he was the one who brought in new business. It was his fantastic connections that created most of the clientele and made their partnership a financial success. He had never mentioned marriage again since that night at the costume party. When she finally told him about Lord Deane's coming marriage, Peter seemed to accept the idea that she could not have continued there. That if the marriage between Brenda and Edan really took place, Maggie could not possibly have stayed on as the decorator. Although no announcement of an engagement had been made, it would probably come at Christmas, Maggie thought—when she could bear to think of it at all.

She and Peter had a long and difficult meeting about her work at Deane Park—the actual hours, the value of her ideas. That was quite a separate matter and had nothing to do with personalities. Finally Peter submitted a bill, but there had been no reply from Edan. Peter, however, did not seem unduly worried. He assured her that Edan would honor his commitment.

Now, with the restaurant opening little more than a week away, Maggie felt the need for a brief holiday. She had worked hard, and she was tired. At the very end, there would be a million details to take care of and she needed refueling. A weekend away, far from London, might just give her the necessary impetus.

"I think I'll go away this weekend," she told Peter on a particularly gloomy Thursday. Looking out on Mount Street, she saw that it was drizzling again. It was almost dark, although it was not yet five o'clock.

"You do look tired," Peter agreed. "If a holiday will give you a lift, why not?"

She was grateful when he did not argue. The decoration had progressed to a point where she could afford to leave the city. The workmen would be off on Saturday and Sunday anyway, and if she came back some time Monday she would have plenty of time to supervise the last-minute details.

"Where were you thinking of going? Paris?"

"I don't care much for Paris when I'm alone. I was thinking of renting a cottage I used to see when I lived at Deane Park. It's beside an inn on the river, and they apparently rent it out. It has privacy and you can take meals at the inn. What I really want is a good rest."

Peter looked doubtful.

"Isn't that a bit close to Deane Park?"

"Oh, there's no need to worry about running into Edan Deane, if that's what you're thinking. He wouldn't go near the inn, it isn't his style."

"I see. Well, I suppose you know what you're doing."

"It's a place I've seen, that's all. I liked it and it isn't far to drive. I don't want to drive for hours and hours."

"It seems odd, that's all. I happen to be driving down that way myself," Peter said casually. "I've been talking to Brenda Hawke on the telephone and I think I've just about convinced her to refurbish some of the rooms in Chagford Hunt. She's invited me down to discuss it."

Maggie felt a quiver of anger at the mere mention of

that name. Which was, she told herself quickly, ridiculous under the circumstances.

"I think she's a skinflint, so good luck. She'll never pay *your* prices, Peter. I suppose if she's willing to redecorate the place, the happy couple must plan to live there."

"She didn't say."

That would leave Deane Park empty. After all her work to restore it, and all Edan's money, too! What a shame. The idea of that beautiful house standing empty once more was depressing.

One call had assured her she could rent the cottage for the weekend, and the innkeeper promised it would be ready for occupancy. And as it happened, the weather was lovely. The trees were now bare of leaves, and there was a carpet of gold and brown in the woods. Here and there, a splash of green suggested cedars or pine. She found the cottage cosy and comfortable. A fire burned in the grate and, as she sank down before it, she was relieved to see that she did not even have to ring for tea. There was a tray waiting for her.

But being in the area made her thoughts turn automatically to Deane Park. She felt excited for no apparent reason. Certainly, she did not intend to go near the place, although she would love to visit Rex and Quinn at the stables. But if she accidentally ran into Edan, it would look as though she regretted leaving. He would be sure to get the wrong idea. No, she must resist that temptation.

Between the inn and the river was a churchyard cemetery. The Bull could only be approached by walking through the graveyard, and it was this oddity that gave the place its special appeal from outside. Inside, the pub was low-ceilinged and heavily beamed. It was one of the oldest in the area, a leftover from Elizabethan times, according to the local historians.

She spent the remainder of Saturday walking along the river and reading some of the inscriptions on the tombstones. After a substantial dinner of meat pie and tea, she decided to linger in the pub with a whisky and soda. The locals were friendly and the atmosphere welcoming. A fire blazing away in the grate was too attractive to resist.

After this one whisky, she told herself, she would retire to her cottage and read one of the books she had brought down. Her feeling of serenity was jarred, however, when she saw Quinn come in, accompanied by the girl she had met in the gypsy camp. They both looked very grave, as if they had been having a serious discussion. She watched as Quinn went to the bar and ordered his drinks. Should she speak to him? When he carried two mugs of beer to his table, Quinn glanced in her direction, and a look of surprise and then pleasure spread over his dark face. He came toward her quickly.

"Miss Jordan! Whatever are you doing in these parts?"

"Hello, Quinn. It's a surprise to see you in here! I didn't know you were a customer at The Bull."

"Not very often, Miss. But we're having a little talk about our future plans. Do you remember Meta? She told your fortune that night at the camp."

"Of course, I remember. But Quinn . . . you aren't leaving Deane Park, are you?"

Edan would be desolate if he left. Quinn had become so much a part of the place. Edan had come to rely on him. But of course, if Edan and Brenda planned to live at Chagford Hunt, that meant Deane Park would be much less active.

"I don't want to, Miss Jordan, but there are reasons . . ."

"Quinn, may I join you for a few moments? I'd like to hear about Deane Park. I'll just finish this drink, and then I'm going back to the cottage. I've rented it for the weekend."

"Of course, Miss. We'd like it if you did."

He carried her glass over to his own table, and she sat down with them. She thought Meta looked sad and wondered what the trouble was, but mostly she wanted to catch up on the news about the estate.

"Is . . . everything all right over there? Lord Deane is well? How about Rex?"

"Oh, he's well enough, I suppose, although I must say he looks a bit peaked-like. He's working too hard. Rex is fine but I think he misses you. Won't you be coming back to finish the work?"

"I don't think so," she said solemnly. "I wish I could. But it doesn't look that way at the moment. But Quinn, why do *you* look so serious? Is it any problem I could help with?"

He exchanged looks with Meta, and then as if by silent consent he said slowly, "Meta thinks I ought to go back to the band. That way, we could get married. As it is, well, it just isn't possible. There's no accommodation over the stables for a married man. And I haven't the money to buy a house."

"If he's with the band," Meta said quickly, "we wouldn't need a house. We could get married and he could live like the others. It's all so different, Miss. But this way, with him being over at the Park, well, we just *can't*. And the others are planning to move along soon, too far away for us to see each other very often."

"Oh, I'm sorry to hear that," Maggie said.

"It's a hard decision to make," Quinn said heavily. "I enjoy the life on the estate. You know that, Miss. But I want to marry Meta, too."

"Lord Deane will be very sorry to lose you," Maggie said. "I know it. But, unfortunately, I don't see him these days, so there's no way I could discuss the problem with him. Why don't you tell him yourself, Quinn?"

"In *his* mood, he wouldn't like it," Quinn said glumly. "I'd be afraid to bring up anything but business, he's that gloomy."

Hardly the description of an ardent bridegroom, Maggie thought, but then she corrected herself. Perhaps it wasn't the marriage that worried Edan, but the thought that he, too, had to make a decision. To give up his lifelong wish to live in Deane Park. How he must hate to have to move to Chagford Hunt!

"I wish I could think of something," she told Quinn, rising from the table. "But I can't. I don't know what to tell you to do."

"Miss, let me see your hand again!" Meta said suddenly.

"Oh, no, really," Maggie protested. She didn't want to know the future. It looked too bleak. Even if she believed in such things, and she *didn't,* of course, she wasn't eager to hear Meta's prediction.

"I didn't really finish reading your hand last time," the girl said.

"That's true. Well, all right."

Maggie sat down again and held out her hands. Meta took them and peered down for some time before she spoke.

"Yes, it has changed. The dark man has gone, and the pretty woman, too."

That was true. No more Byron and Lady Caroline! What did it all matter to her now, whether they had ever visited Deane Park?

"I see sadness here. And loneliness, at least for a little while. Oh, and illness. Not you, Miss, but someone close to you. But . . . if you remain true to your own ideals, it will all work out. I'm sure it will."

Maggie thanked her, but she was certain the girl was

wrong. Nothing was ever going to work out for her
again. She was sad and she was lonely, and nothing
would ever be the same. She wished she had never
come to Deane Park. That she had never taken the
assignment in the first place. That she had never met
Edan Deane.

For the remainder of the weekend it rained sporadically and she stayed indoors with her books. Several
times she was tempted to drive over to Deane Park to
see Rex and take him for a run, but she resisted. She
would never, never let Edan Deane see how much she
cared about the Park, how much she missed the life
there!

Back in London, she threw herself into the final days
of preparations on The Folly with renewed vigor. She
tried to stamp out all thoughts of Edan Deane and of
the lush and rolling acres of the estate. All longings for
Rex, and all visions of Quinn and his problems and how
he might leave and return to his people. She would
never see the little painting again either, nor the harp,
nor Lady Amalie's journals. Only the fact that she kept
busy prevented her from crying.

The party was a success. Everyone on the guest list
who was really important turned up. One of the
columnists who carried a great deal of weight promised
a review of the restaurant, and there was even a
photographer from *Country Life* magazine. Peter said
the restaurant was off to an excellent start, no question
about it. From now on, he pronounced, it was up to the
chef and the ambience that the owner could manage to
create.

It was after two when she got back to Cheyne Walk.
Peter drove her home but did not ask to come in, and
she was glad. She wanted to go to sleep. To forget.

But instead of flinging herself into bed, she found a

man on her doorstep. It was a moment before she realized who it was.

"Why, Quinn! What are you doing in London?"

"Sorry, Miss, if I frightened you. But I had to see you. I thought about this a lot, and then I decided to just come. To tell you what I have to say."

She was a bit startled, but she let him in.

"We had an opening tonight. A restaurant I designed. So I'm a bit tired."

"I won't keep you too long, Miss. Maybe I'm out of place, coming here like this. But I didn't know what else to do. I couldn't tell you on the telephone."

She offered him a drink but he refused.

"No, thank you. I'll just speak my piece."

"What's wrong, Quinn? You haven't decided to leave Deane Park, have you?"

"Oh, no, Miss. Not that."

"And Rex? You still have the dog?"

"Rex is fine, Miss. Oh, yes, there's nothing the matter with Rex. It's Lord Deane. It's him that I'm worried about. And nobody can do nothing with him. And if he goes on like this, he'll fall sick. He's sick now, if you ask me, but he won't quit."

"Edan is sick?"

She felt ill herself at the news. She sat down abruptly, opposite Quinn, in the elegant drawing room, and said, shakily, "Tell me about Lord Deane."

"I thought you'd want to know." Quinn said, wisely. "And maybe, just *maybe,* you can do something about it. It's worse since I talked to you last Saturday. Lord Deane works night and day. He hardly stops to eat. He drives everybody else, too. But that don't worry me as much as himself. He's lost so much weight. Well, if you don't stop to eat, you lose weight. He's gloomy. He's cranky. And he works, works, works. Well, he looks terrible."

"I see. What about Miss Hawke? Doesn't she try to talk to him?"

"She comes over, yes. But whatever she says, I don't know. It makes no difference, whatever it is. Because still he works on and on. Half the night, up first thing, and at it again. He's into everything—the sheep, the tenants, rebuilding fences, repairing the stables. I don't know the half of it. Now he's tearing away at the stone bridge. Says it isn't safe. Well, it's been like that for as long as Lord Deane has been alive, if you ask me. And it won't fall down now. But he's got a team of stone masons on it."

"And he doesn't eat?"

"Hardly ever eats. Hasn't time, he tells me. 'No time for lunch, Quinn,' he says, 'I've got work to do.' Well, he looks awful. I think he's sickening for something. He has a cough."

"A bad cough?"

"Sounds bad to me. I said, 'Get the doctor and let him give you medicine for that cough, your Lordship,' but he don't listen. 'I'm all right, perfectly all right,' he says. And goes on working."

"Oh, Quinn, I had no idea things were so awful when we talked the other night. But what can I possibly do? I'm not even employed there anymore. But surely Miss Hawke can talk some sense into Lord Deane. After all, he's *her* responsibility now."

"She doesn't seem to try, Miss. And that's another thing that worries me," Quinn said, frowning down at his hands in an uncomfortable way. "It isn't my place to say this, but there's something odd about the house. I don't have much cause to go up there, but the other day, when I was talking to Bateman about something, I happened to be inside. And I noticed that all the doors were closed. It wasn't natural. Not in a house like that."

"You mean the doors to the reception rooms?"

"That's right, Miss. The door to the library, and the dining room, and all the others. Closed off. With the central heating, I always understood it was best to keep the warm air flowing. To circulate it. But that's not what's happening. It was like a funeral parlor. And Mrs. Bateman says they've been closed since you left."

Maggie had a startling thought. Edan Deane missed her! And this was his way of closing off the memories. But then a more plausible explanation sprang to mind.

"That's Brenda Hawke's idea!" she cried. "I'm sure it must be. She hated the way I redecorated the house. She doesn't want Lord Deane to see the rooms I worked on."

"Yes, I suppose that could be it."

There was a long silence while each sat thinking about the problem, and then Maggie asked, "What do you think I could do, Quinn?"

"That's just it. I don't know. It was only a feeling. I thought sometimes, when I saw you and Lord Deane talking, that you liked each other. I remember watching you go off the night of the costume party over at Chagford, and I thought . . . those two ought to be together."

"Oh, no, you're quite wrong about that, Quinn. He's going to marry Miss Hawke. They've known each other for a long time. They have the same interests. And anyway, I have my career and it's going very well. I love London. I want to live here."

The words had begun to sound hollow even to herself. Why did she find it necessary to keep saying that?

"No doubt I was wrong to come here. I shouldn't try to interfere. I'll be going along now. But if you do happen to reconsider, well, Miss, I'm sure you could think of a reason to visit Deane Park and see for yourself. *Some* excuse. If you talked it over with him, you might be able to make him see some common sense. And Rex would like to see you," he added hopefully.

"And I'd like to see Rex," she said with genuine feeling. "I'll think about what you've said, Quinn. I can't promise more than that."

"Thank you, Miss. I know it's late. I'll be going."

He rose and moved toward the door.

"Do you have a place to stay tonight, Quinn?"

"Thank you, yes. I have friends in London. There are gypsies everywhere, you know." He gave her a brief smile to indicate there were no hard feelings. As she watched him go downstairs, a wistful sensation almost overwhelmed her. If only she had some logical reason to go back! If only she could make it appear casual. But it would probably seem a flimsy pretext, whatever she said.

Of course, there was the unpaid bill. Professional designers like Peter and herself did not collect their own bills. But she could pretend that she thought he was quarrelling with the bill and that's why he had been slow to pay. She could tell him that if he disagreed with any of the items, perhaps they could talk it over and make an adjustment.

She tried to visualize the scene. Would it sound too thin? She desperately wanted to see the house again, and the park, and Rex. It seemed years since she had actually been on the estate. She owed it to Edan to try to cheer him up, didn't she?

She wrestled with the scheme all weekend. At times she imagined Edan so ill that he had to be taken to hospital in an ambulance. Not having eaten properly, and working so hard, his resistance was undoubtedly low. Perhaps he was slowly dying. And a woman like Brenda wouldn't even notice. She was so preoccupied with herself, she had no time for anyone's problems. By the time two days had elapsed, Maggie had made herself too ill to work, too restless to concentrate, and too disorganized to accomplish anything worthwhile.

On Monday she packed a small bag and climbed into the red convertible, determined to do something. The long drive to Deane Park, which had become so familiar, seemed extraordinarily short. Part of her was anxious to arrive, but the other part was afraid that Edan Deane would reject her visit. That he would see through her ruse.

She actually passed the entrance to Chagford Hunt and felt a sharp pang of fear and dislike. At the stone gates of Deane Park she turned in, feeling nervous and a trifle ill. What if Edan dismissed her? As she drove over the stone bridge, reading again the little sign Edan had put up warning people about the lambs, she saw that repairs were still going on. What did that mean? That he intended to rent the place once he moved to Chagford?

Then the house rose up before her, a colder pink in the gray November light and surrounded now by trees stripped bare of leaves. The grass was a pallid brown. Still, the place looked lovely—graceful and welcoming. There was a car in the driveway that she did not recognize. So Edan had guests.

Again she wondered if she ought to retreat before she made a fool of herself. As she hesitated before the doorbell, a surge of loneliness came over her and she knew that she must see him. Surely it couldn't do any harm to see Edan for a little while?

Mrs. Bateman opened the door to her and looked completely taken aback.

"Why, Miss Jordan! How did you know?"

"Know what? Is something the matter?"

She found she could scarcely speak; her nerves were

stretched so tight that she almost pushed past Mrs. Bateman to get in. Something was definitely wrong here.

"His Lordship is ill. Doctor Baker is up there with him now. He's just run himself into the ground, Miss. But nobody could tell him. He wouldn't listen."

"But what does the doctor say?" Her voice was dry, the words difficult to get out. "I didn't know he was sick. I came for another reason . . . but that doesn't matter, now."

"He's got something the matter with his chest," Mrs. Bateman told her. "He's been coughing for days. I've been telling him to eat, to get some sleep. But he's like a wild man." She shook her head.

"I'll talk to the doctor when he comes down," Maggie said. "Here, take my coat, please."

"Would you like some tea while you wait?"

"No, I can't—I mean, I'm not hungry. I'll just wait. Why are all the doors closed? It looks awful. And that's not good for the restoration, Mrs. Bateman."

"He told me to shut them. There isn't a fire in any of the grates. That was his orders. 'Close them up,' he said, 'I don't want to see them.' I tell you, Miss Jordan, he's acting strange. We've all been worried."

She was about to ask for a fire in the rent room, but at that moment Doctor Baker came down the stairs carrying his bag.

"Ah, Mrs. Bateman, there you are. He's got bronchitis. And if he doesn't take care, it'll go into pneumonia. Now, he's got to stay in bed with plenty of hot water bottles, and a fire in that grate, please. I've got two prescriptions here to be filled. Send Bateman, will you? The next thing is, he needs a nurse. The best I can do is try in the village, but I doubt I can find anybody willing to come before morning. Now, who's this?" He looked at Maggie questioningly.

"I'm a friend, Doctor. Maggie Jordan. I was in charge of the restoration here."

"You're not a nurse, then?"

"No, but I can help, Doctor. I'm quite good at it."

"Staying overnight, Miss Jordan? If so, you can certainly see that Lord Deane takes his medicine. And that he has the hot water bottles I've ordered."

"Yes, I'm staying," she said, suddenly making up her mind. "You can depend on me, Doctor. I'll see he gets the medicine."

"Lord Deane is a difficult man. You may have trouble with him. But I'll send a nurse out as soon as I can get one to take the case," Doctor Baker said, hurrying toward the door. "Call me, if you have any trouble. And get that room warmed up! I don't know if he thinks he can solve the energy crisis all by himself, but this house is damned cold!"

And he bustled off.

Maggie followed Mrs. Bateman to the kitchen. She filled two hot water bottles and listened while Mrs. Bateman sent Bateman to the village for the medical supplies. Then she carried the heating equipment up to Edan's bedroom and quietly opened the door.

He was lying propped up against pillows, a box of tissues beside him, and a quilt pulled up to his chin. He was coughing still, although Mrs. Bateman whispered to Maggie that she thought the doctor had given him something in a needle. Maggie noticed that he was distinctly drowsy.

"Here," she said brightly. "Let me put these in the bottom of the bed."

He glared at her, disbelieving.

"What are *you* doing here?"

"That's not much of a welcome," she said, poking the hot water bottles under the covers. "Does that feel better?"

He began to cough. He looked exhausted and, now

that she had a chance to examine him closer, much thinner.

"Have you come back just so you can leave again?" he demanded. "I don't like cowards who run away."

She was about to protest that she had left for a good reason—his coming marriage to Brenda Hawke. But the medicine the doctor had given him took effect and he drowsed off. Mrs. Bateman came in at that moment, to build up the fire.

"I'll stay here until the pills arrive. When he wakes, I'll see that he takes them," Maggie said. "And I would like some tea now, Mrs. Bateman."

"Of course, Miss. I'm just glad you're here. I wouldn't want to take the responsibility myself."

By the time Edan wakened, it was evening. Maggie had the pills ready and a glass of water to help them down. He looked at her groggily.

"I don't want you here," Edan said. "So you can leave."

But he took the pills and the water and sank back into the pillows. She made him sip some warm tea.

"Fluids. You need fluids. You have a high temperature," Maggie said professionally, touching his forehead. "Some juice, too, would be a good idea."

"Do you think you're an actress?" he demanded angrily, beginning to cough. "From decorator to Lady Caroline to Miss Nightingale."

The coughing prevented an argument, and again he lay back looking tired and furious.

"Doctor Baker is sending a nurse out tomorrow," Maggie said, trying to be patient because he was so ill. "You won't have to put up with my presence for long. In the meantime, I'll stay. You can't expect Mrs. Bateman to look after you."

He fell asleep again. The medicine seemed to add to his drowsiness. That and the fact that he was totally exhausted, Maggie thought. She went to her old room and unpacked the small bag Bateman had carried up for her. She had decided, whether it was proper or not, to sleep on the chaise longue in Edan's room. This way, she could give him his pills when he woke in the night and also keep the fire stoked. With this in mind, she brought a pillow and a quilt from her bedroom to Edan's apartment.

All through the following day, she stayed with him. He swung often from sleeping to waking and coughed a great deal. She forced him to take cough medicine, as well as the pills the doctor had prescribed. She also tried to make him drink liquids, and she replaced the hot water bottles frequently to keep him warm. When Doctor Baker called the next day, he found some improvement, but reported that he could not find a nurse to take over the case.

"Everybody in the county is sick," he complained. "So all the available nurses are busy. Can you possibly stay on, Miss Jordan? At least for another few days?"

"Well, I suppose I could. I'll have to call my office and tell them what's happened. I'm supposed to be going on another assignment."

"I'm sorry, but I don't know what else to suggest," the doctor said, putting on his coat to leave. "It's awkward for you, I'm sure."

"I won't leave while he needs me," she said.

She wondered if she ought to mention Brenda to Edan when he was awake. Surely since Brenda was his fiancée she ought to be notified that he was sick. *She* was the one who ought to be here nursing him. But Edan didn't ask for Brenda, and Maggie was reluctant to yield her favored position to her rival. No, she decided, if Brenda didn't bother to telephone or call at the house, she couldn't miss Edan very much and she wasn't terribly concerned. What kind of engagement did they have, anyway?

Within two days, Doctor Baker pronounced Lord

Deane definitely on the mend. But he was to remain in bed resting and taking his medication for at least a week. He must also begin to eat regular meals.

Edan had recovered enough to argue and his first act was to order Maggie out of his room. She was to stop sleeping on the chaise, and he was perfectly capable of taking his own pills, he said. He did not need her charity.

Perhaps he was sulking about Brenda, Maggie thought. He must have noticed that Brenda did not call or visit. That would be very hurtful if he really cared about her.

As for his orders that she retreat from the room, she simply froze him with a look and changed his hot water bottle. Nevertheless, she now felt that she had time to talk to Quinn and have a friendly visit with Rex. So far she hadn't left the sickroom long enough to take so much as a stroll.

"I'm going out to the stables to see the dog," she said to Edan by way of explanation. "I trust you haven't gotten rid of him just because he doesn't like your friend Miss Hawke?"

"He's still there as far as I know," Edan said grumpily. "I have never considered getting rid of Rex. I like the dog. Besides, old Farraday would be upset if he heard."

She put on woollen trousers and her short winter jacket, with its sheepskin lining, and tied a scarf around her head. It was cold, and even a short walk to the stables required warm clothing. She found Quinn in the tack room mending a saddle. He stopped as soon as she came in and greeted her, his dark gypsy face expressing pleasure at her presence.

"I heard you'd come," he said.

Before they could talk further, Rex was leaping at her, making sounds of welcome. She hugged him and finally calmed him down.

"That's a better welcome than I got from your master," she told the dog. She laughed, but at the same time the truth of it stung.

"Bateman says Lord Deane is getting better," Quinn said. "I knew you could help, Miss."

"He practically threw me out this morning," she said, "so I don't know how much help I've been. Except to Mrs. Bateman. I think she's delighted there's somebody to take half the orders and the bad temper. Men like Lord Deane are the worst patients in the world."

"You're staying on awhile?" Quin asked tentatively.

"Well, I don't know for how long. He's still angry because I left the job without telling him. I suppose Brenda Hawke will be coming over soon, and when she does I expect she'll insist that I leave."

Quinn looked skeptical.

"Miss Hawke hasn't been around for days. If she cared, why doesn't she telephone?"

"That's what I say. But then, I wouldn't consider Miss Hawke a suitable fiancée for Lord Deane. So I'm not much of a judge."

After her visit with Quinn and the dog, she went back to the house. Mrs. Bateman had built a fire in the rent room. It was shabby still, but a comfortable place in which to sit.

"I'll have a drink in here, Mrs. Bateman. Tell Bateman I'd like some sherry, please."

"Yes, Miss. Will you take his Lordship's tray up or shall I?"

"His supper tray, you mean? I will. He isn't allowed any whisky when he's taking antibiotics, you know. So no matter what he says, don't give him any alcohol."

"Yes, Miss. You warm up here and I'll see that you get the sherry."

When Mrs. Bateman came back, she said, "His

Lordship's tray will be ready in twenty minutes. I hope that's all right with you, Miss."

"Yes, that's fine. Mrs. Bateman, when Miss Hawke was here last, did they—well, were there words? An argument of some kind? I find it hard to believe she wouldn't call. Or visit."

Mrs. Bateman hesitated. Gossiping was against her policy, and she had always been careful to keep her opinions to herself. But under questioning she admitted there had been a tiff of sorts.

"Miss Hawke told his Lordship that all the rooms would have to be done over. That none of them—well, she said you'd done them all wrong, Miss Jordan."

"I see. And what did he say?"

"He shouted at her. Told her to mind her own business. Then she started in about the story concerning Lady Caroline Lamb's visit here all those years ago. A bunch of nonsense, she said. The painting wasn't real, either. You just wanted to believe it was."

"Oh, dear. He wouldn't like her telling him what to do," Maggie said, with a touch of fondness that did not escape Mrs. Bateman's attention.

"No, he doesn't like to be told. A woman would have to be clever to manage his Lordship," Mrs. Bateman said, and then added slyly, "I've always thought *you* could handle him, Miss."

Maggie blushed. "That's never been the issue, Mrs. Bateman. He asked Miss Hawke to marry him, not me."

"He did?" She seemed astonished. "I didn't hear about it."

"I'm surprised the word didn't get out," Maggie said uncertainly. "I thought they would have announced it by this time. Perhaps that argument slowed things."

"Are you sure? About the proposal?"

"I heard him myself," Maggie said quickly, and then realizing how peculiar that sounded she went on, "I mean, I was about to walk into a room a long time ago—and they were there. And I heard him say something about accepting her proposal."

"Ah, so *she* proposed," Mrs. Bateman said. "That sounds more like it."

"Yes, but he accepted, that's the point."

Now that the words were said aloud, it sounded less certain. She had heard him accept, but it was true that Brenda must have made the actual proposal. Somehow, that made her feel better.

"It's not my business, anyway. He's trying to send me away. . . . I'll take that tray when it's ready, Mrs. Bateman."

She knocked and entered the room, bearing the tray. He was sitting up in bed, a velour robe draped around him to keep his shoulders warm. He still looked drawn, but there was more color in his cheeks.

"So you're still doing guard duty, are you?" he said crossly. "I thought I sent you packing."

"Sick people are notably weak-minded."

"*I'm* not. Don't I get any wine?"

"No alcohol with antibiotics. You know perfectly well what Doctor Baker said."

"I'd like at least a glass of sherry," he demanded. "It's miserable enough being sick."

"The alcohol cancels out the antibiotics. They don't work as well," she said, as if she were explaining to a child. "So just eat your soup."

"I'm not an idiot. You needn't speak to me in that ridiculous tone. I understand what Baker said, but I want a drink anyway."

"Well, you aren't having one."

She stirred up the fire, turning her back on him. Really, he was like a spoiled child. She wouldn't have been surprised if he'd thrown the soup on the floor.

"I had no idea you were so bossy, Miss Jordan.

. . . How's the decorating business? Doing any exciting castles now that you've left me in the lurch?"

"No. I did a restaurant recently, though."

"And it was a smashing success, I suppose?"

"People said so, yes."

"So you're going on with your career? More and better drawing rooms, is that it? Bigger and richer houses? I got Peter's bill, by the way. I'll pay it as soon as I have time. It's not the expense I mind, I always honor my commitments."

"That's what Peter said. He isn't worried. . . . What *do* you mind?"

"I mind people starting things they don't finish."

"Brenda Hawke didn't like what I did here. So there was no use going on."

"It isn't Brenda's house. Or have you not grasped that fundamental fact yet?"

"Oh, what's the use! I'm leaving as soon as possible—tomorrow, if you don't really need a nurse. When Doctor Baker comes, you might ask him if you can go downstairs for meals, and if you can manage to take your own pills."

"I'll ask him. Go ahead and leave me. You usually do desert when the going gets rough. I've noticed it."

"You are impossible! You're a tyrant, and you're rude and you think you only have to look at a girl to have her fall on her back in bed. You're horrible. I told you that before, and I say it again. I'm leaving. Tomorrow."

"Good. I'm glad. I don't know why you came back. I didn't ask you to come. I wouldn't beg anybody to come back. And that includes you, Miss Jordan. Though you've left my house in a mess, I refuse to beg, or even command you. And you still insist that *I* am bossy and impossible!"

"I don't suggest—I *know*. You believe women are second-class. You told me so. It seems a lifetime ago that you said women ought to give up careers for marriage. Well, I won't. I love my work. I love my work and I hate *you!*"

She was shouting. She knew that she was almost in tears and that would be the final disgrace. To let Edan see her cry when she was furious.

"You're the stupidest woman I've ever met!"

At that, Maggie marched out of the room, shouting as she went, "I'll send Mrs. Bateman. Perhaps you can act sensibly toward her, for a change."

She did not go near him that night, even to check on whether or not he had taken all his pills. Not even with a hot water bottle. She spent a restless night, and when she woke up, somewhere around dawn, she knew she must leave. But first, she would do one decent thing. Which was more than Edan Deane would have done for her.

She would drive over to Chagford Hunt and inform Brenda Hawke about his sickness. At least, they couldn't say she had pulled some trick, and Brenda couldn't blame her later. Let Brenda take over the sickroom, and the decorating, and everything connected with Deane Park. And good riddance to all of them!

Chapter Ten

Once more she packed her bag and went downstairs before anyone was awake, and once more she walked out to the stable to say goodbye to Quinn and Rex. It was cold. She bundled into her sheepskin jacket, and still she shivered a bit.

Quinn came out, looking frustrated and puzzled.

"You're leaving? But you've helped his Lordship so much," he protested. "I thought you'd be here all winter, Miss."

"Here all winter? Lord Deane is impossible, Quinn! I know I shouldn't say that to you, because you work for him and you want to stay on here. But he's mad, I tell you. I did all I could—" She broke off, and shrugged helplessly.

"But he did get better fast," Quinn pointed out.

She hugged Rex once again and felt the same reluctance to leave him. She always seemed to be saying goodbye to Quinn and the dog. It was becoming a habit.

"Just his good constitution, I expect," she said. "Anyway, last night he said he'd be glad to see me leave. So I'm going. There's no reason why I should stay here and take abuse."

"No, Miss. I agree. But it's a great pity he can't control his temper."

And his passions, Maggie amended silently, thinking again of those times when Edan had swept her off her feet.

"Goodbye then, Quinn."

"Have you told Mrs. Bateman you're leaving?"

"No, I haven't. You're the only one. And I don't want you to tell anyone yet. They'll find out soon enough. I want to get back to London before Lord Deane realizes I'm gone. That way, I'll feel safe."

She would stop off at Chagford to tell Brenda Hawke about Edan's illness, and at the same time to suggest that perhaps she'd like to take over the nursing chores. Doctor Baker had been unsuccessful in finding a nurse, since everyone in the area seemed to have an invalid in the house. And now that Edan was feeling better, he wouldn't require much more than a companion. Someone to encourage him to take his pills and stay warm and eat properly. Surely Brenda would not be too selfish to do that much.

Chagford was stirring by the time she arrived. The butler showed her to a small sitting room, suggesting that she have coffee while she waited. She was more than willing to take him up on that suggestion and was drinking her second cup when Brenda breezed in.

"Miss Jordan? This *is* a surprise! I didn't realize you were still around."

Brenda looked elegant, dressed in a woollen pant suit and turtle-neck sweater in a heather color that was most flattering. Quite the mistress of the castle, Maggie thought with envy. Rich, and beautiful, and very secure. No wonder she could treat Edan with such casualness.

"I'm on my way back to London," Maggie explained, keeping her temper. She was determined to do the right thing: to let Brenda know, and then leave her to pick up the pieces. "I've been at Deane Park on business, but I thought you should know that Edan has been ill. He's still sick, and since you and he are—well, practically engaged—I feel you will want to visit him. If you'd telephoned, of course, I would have told you sooner, but—"

"I had no idea Edan was ill. I've been terribly busy here, with plans for restoring sections of the house, and buying cattle, and organizing the hunt."

Naturally, Brenda would be bossing the local hunt, Maggie thought. You could count on women like her to ride to hounds, to enjoy all the rituals that went with these ancient and established packs.

"He had bronchitis. The doctor thought it might turn into pneumonia. Edan hasn't been eating properly and he's been working too hard. He's very rundown. I'm surprised you didn't notice. I mean, if you intend to marry him—"

Brenda gave her a hard look, and Maggie knew that she was on shaky ground. But exactly why wasn't clear.

"Why do you think I'm going to marry Edan Deane?"

Brenda poured herself a coffee from the pot on the silver tray and carefully fixed it to suit her taste. As with everything she did, there was an air of deliberation, of knowing exactly what she wanted and how to achieve it.

"You implied as much many times, Miss Hawke. And I thought everything was decided the night of the costume party. Wasn't it?"

Brenda looked amazed.

"I don't know what you mean. Edan and I were

together, but other than that—oh yes, we *did* make one important decision! I asked Edan to be Master of Hounds for the South Chagford Hunt. And he accepted. I was delighted, of course—we have so few men capable of taking on the job. It's so important. Historically, we've had long and continuous Mastership here at Chagford, and we need to find a man who is likely to be in the area for many years. A young man, too. Edan is perfect for the role. Major Blunt, who was our Master for ten years, is leaving because he's been elected to the National Chairmanship of the Pony Club. So, naturally, I thought of Edan and I asked him. But how did you know about this?"

Maggie blushed.

"I was looking for Peter. I came to the library door and you had just asked Edan something and he said, 'Since you propose it, I believe I will.' So, of course, I thought—"

"That I had *proposed marriage* to Edan?"

Brenda laughed. Not with much mirth, however. It was rather a brittle, cold laugh, and she looked insulted.

"Yes. I thought you had proposed and he had accepted."

"I see. You don't know much about human nature, do you, Miss Jordan? Or about me? The last thing in the world I would do is propose to a man like Edan Deane."

"But you did seem to—well, you *behaved* in such a way that anyone would think you wanted to marry him. . . . You can't deny that, Miss Hawke. I watched you."

"Perhaps," Brenda said noncommittally. "I thought at one time it would be a perfect solution. What a superb estate we would have, if we joined forces! And Edan is attractive. But he would never move here to Chagford, for one thing. He thinks that Deane Park is heaven on earth. At the same time, *I* love Chagford. I couldn't live anywhere else. I had to face that fact. That's the reason it's taken me so long to decide whether or not to spend money on this place—" She waved her hands to indicate the huge house. "But I realized, after a great deal of thought, that I could never move. I must stay here and rebuild Chagford Hunt. As a matter of fact, I've arranged for the renovations with your employer, Peter Cross."

As she spoke, Peter came in. It was obvious that he had spent the night in the house and that he had come down looking for breakfast. He wore cords and a lightweight pullover, just the clothes for a country visit, Maggie noticed, and he had his pipe in his hand.

"Is there any coffee, my love?" he asked Brenda, before he spotted Maggie. "I've had nothing so far but some weak tea and that won't wake me up, I'm afraid. You'll have to do something about that cook, my sweet. She's simply *too* medieval. Coffee is the civilized thing these days . . ."

He broke off suddenly, having noticed Maggie.

"Why, Maggie ! What are you doing here? I had no idea you'd left London."

"I couldn't seem to find you at the office when I called," Maggie said. "I've been in this area for a few days."

She had caught the mood between these two and realized that Peter and Brenda were more than employer and employee. There was a genuine, easy communication between them. From the look of things, Peter had the run of the house and could tell Brenda what he thought about her cook without insulting his hostess.

"I'm afraid I neglected to keep you up-to-date. Brenda and I have been working out an agreement on some much-needed repairs here. A great deal of the panelling must be restored before it peels off and is good for nothing but firewood. I was telling Brenda she's fortunate I came along. Another year or two and the house would be beyond help."

"Well, you said you were coming down to talk to Miss Hawke, but I had no idea things had gone so far," Maggie said. "I came to see her about a personal matter."

"Yes," Brenda said brightly. "Miss Jordan had the idea I was going to marry Edan. Isn't that interesting? Do have some of this coffee, Peter, so you'll be ready to begin work. We have so much to do this morning. I'll see what cook has prepared for breakfast."

No wonder Peter had stayed at Chagford Hunt, if this was the kind of attention he got from Brenda. What could be cosier? A potentially lucrative assignment and a beautiful, pampering hostess! He certainly had figured out that Brenda wasn't engaged. She supposed he had other things on his mind than informing her of that fact. He hadn't even bothered to take back his proposal to her. Probably he had forgotten all about it by now. Not that she had ever seriously entertained the idea of marrying Peter Cross. As a matter of fact, she had thought recently that she might never marry at all. She might make interior design her whole life.

As for poor Edan, he would have to look after himself. Brenda was obviously abandoning him, and she, Maggie, was returning to London. Well, it served him right for being such a tyrant. What he did was no longer of any concern to her. He could stay in Deane Park and turn into a hermit for all she cared. Brenda and Peter would no doubt spend a perfectly lovely winter restoring Chagford, while Maggie would be working in London on a mews house for some plump dowager with absolutely no taste and far too much money. That was apparently her destiny.

"I must go. I want to be back in London before noon," Maggie said, setting down her cup.

"Sure you won't stay for breakfast?" Brenda invited, but with no encouragement.

"Thank you, no. If you need me, Peter, you can reach me at the office. Oh, by the way, you might like to know that your friend Lord Deane has been quite ill. Perhaps you'd like to visit him. If you have time, of course."

"Oh, I'm sorry to hear that. I'll give him a call soon. And if you need me, just ring me up here. I'll be at Chagford for a few days, by the look of things."

Yes, I'll call you, Peter, if I need you desperately, but not otherwise. You've just landed the nicest little assignment of your career if I read the signs correctly. While I must go back to London and cope with the clients all on my own.

She caught herself in the midst of this bitter thinking as she climbed into the Morris and turned the key. As the car purred along the throughway, she brought herself up short. Why complain? She would have a free hand with the business while Peter was so absorbed. He'd have little time for other clients and she could pick and choose. It was perfect, really. It would definitely forward her career.

Then why wasn't she gloriously happy?

When she answered that question honestly, she found that she longed for Deane Park. Living in the country, far from being boring as she had always expected it would be, had been a beautiful and exciting experience. The house was the loveliest one she was ever likely to restore. She had enjoyed riding, too, with Quinn as a teacher. And she loved Rex. Then, of course, there was the volatile Lord Deane.

Still, she might as well put Deane Park right out of her mind. Even with dear Brenda giving her full attention to Chagford Hunt and Peter Cross, Edan Deane himself had not changed one tiny bit. Every-

thing about him, his temper, his lust, his chauvinism
was the same. Nothing would ever make a dent in such
a personality.

In her own flat again, she changed her clothes and
then made a few telephone calls. After that, she drove
to the office where she spoke to a couple of potential
clients and discussed the overall plan for the mews flat.
By evening she felt exhausted, although it had not been
a particularly difficult day.

She had just retired to bed with a book when the
telephone rang. She jumped. There was no one who
might call her at this hour. What could have happened?
She let it ring three times before picking it up.

To her astonishment, she heard Mrs. Bateman on the
line. And the woman sounded distraught.

"I couldn't believe you'd left us this morning, Miss,"
she said with a tremble in her voice. "I know you
threatened to when his Lordship acted up. But I never
thought you'd really do it."

"I'm sorry, Mrs. Bateman, but he's quite impossible.
I tried my best, but I couldn't do anything with
him."

"When Quinn told me you'd gone, I said he was
daft," Mrs. Bateman went on ignoring Maggie's explanation. "Then I went right to your room and I saw your
bag gone. *He* doesn't know yet. He thinks you've
driven into the village. But you've got to get back
before he finds out, Miss. I can't manage him. And
neither can Bateman."

"Then try Doctor Baker," she said.

Maggie sympathized with Mrs. Bateman. The housekeeper wielded even less authority than Maggie herself.
But she could not bear to think of returning and letting
Edan Deane treat her so roughly again. What was the
point of torturing herself like that?

"I called the doctor and he came over, but all he can

do is tell his Lordship what to do for his health. It's his mood I'm worried about. He's just not doing anything right."

"Whatever do you mean, Mrs. Bateman? Lord Deane was improving when I last saw him."

"He won't eat. He won't take his medicine. He's left his bed, and he won't even drink his tea. He'll slip right back to where he was before, if he doesn't look out! He'll get sicker and sicker."

"Now, don't worry, Mrs. Bateman. Nobody lets himself get that ill deliberately. Not even Lord Deane."

"But that's not all, Miss. He threatens to get rid of the dog. I spoke to Quinn and he's very upset. He says he wants to leave Deane Park, too, and if he does that will only make things worse. What will become of us, if everybody leaves?"

"Lord Deane won't get rid of the dog," Maggie said.

But what if he did? Was he really in such a depressed state that he didn't understand these wild threats? She thought of Rex. His intelligent eyes and his loyal ways. Really, this was too much! She couldn't let anything happen to Rex.

"He says he'll have the dog put down," Mrs. Bateman said, confirming Maggie's own worst fears. "I'm not sure he's in control of himself, Miss Jordan."

She made up her mind right then that she would return to Deane Park. The whole world seemed to be falling apart. She began to wonder if he was delirious, if he might be much more gravely ill than even Doctor Baker realized. At least this time, she didn't have to consider Brenda Hawke's feeling in the matter. And that was some comfort. She could go back until Edan recovered his senses—that would save Rex and make Quinn less restless. Then, once Edan regained his normal view of things, she would resume her life in London.

*   *   *

It was early evening when she was let in by Mrs. Bateman. The woman was delighted to see her and showed Maggie into the rent room. Lord Deane had apparently given up using the refurbished library and had gone right back to the shabby, old room they had commandeered as a substitute, for she found him in front of the fire, staring into the flames. His tea stood untouched on a tray nearby. She saw the painting of the folly nailed recklessly to the wall. It was slightly askew.

When she approached him, he looked up at her with an angry glare.

"This is a fine time to be coming in! Where have you been? Don't you know I've been expecting you all day? You didn't even tell me where you were going. Who is supposed to look after me?"

"I don't have to account to you for every minute," she protested, a little stunned by his attitude.

"Yes, you do. I'm not supposed to be left alone. Doctor Baker says I still need a nurse. What was I to think? What kept you in the village, anyway?"

"Several things," she said vaguely. "That's no way to hang the picture. I told you I'd look after that."

"I wanted to study it. To remind me of a time when you were sensible, when I could trust you, Miss Jordan. Do you remember the storm? The day the roof leaked?"

"Yes, I do. There are some things we must discuss, Edan, if I'm to stay on."

She would have to confess that she had called upon Brenda and the way she had misunderstood their relationship, but she wasn't at all sure this was the right time. He seemed so terribly disturbed.

"Will you have tea, Miss Jordan?" Mrs. Bateman enquired. "There's only one cup on the tray. Perhaps I ought to bring a fresh pot."

"Yes, please. Will you have a cup with me, Edan?"

"I'll have whisky."

"No, you won't. It's bad for you. Did you take your pills?"

Edan began to argue, but finally swallowed the pills she laid out for him. He continued to give her furious looks, however.

"Well, where have you been?"

"I'm about to tell you. First, I paid a call on Brenda Hawke. I felt it was about time and now I'm glad I did. Because at least I found out one thing. I found out she didn't propose to you."

He looked bewildered.

"Propose? What has Brenda Hawke to do with anything? The woman is supposed to be a friend and she hasn't even telephoned for days. Sometimes, Maggie Jordan, I think you've lost your mind."

"And I sometimes think you have. So we agree on yet another point, but there were reasons, you see. I thought I was doing the honorable thing going over there to tell her you were sick. I thought as your fiancée, she ought to be told."

"My fiancée? Brenda Hawke is *not* my fiancée, and never was. What gave you such a ridiculous idea?"

"I know now I was wrong but, you see, the night of the party I overheard her proposal to you and you accepted. Naturally, I assumed it was a proposal of marriage, and . . ."

"You assumed? That sounds like you."

"You admit you said, 'Since you propose it, I believe I will.'"

"You're the silliest woman I've ever met."

"What would anyone think if they had heard that?"

"If they were properly educated, they might recognize it as a quotation. That line is from 'Mr. Flood's Party,' a poem by Edwin Arlington Robinson. I used it as a kind of joke, you see. Miss Hawke asked me to be Master of Hounds for the local hunt," he explained, then added, "So all this time you thought I was engaged to Brenda?"

"It was logical, wasn't it? You and Brenda have so much in common. The estates, side by side, the hunting and riding and friends. Why wouldn't anyone expect you to get married? Not to mention Brenda's flirting."

"I've never thought of her in a romantic way."

"She made plenty of fuss about you at times."

"She may have been trying on the idea, I don't dispute it. I couldn't very well be rude. We're neighbors."

"Why not? You've been rude to me, quite often," she said with a touch of acidity. "For example, when you called me the stupidest woman in the world."

He was suddenly contrite.

"That was unforgivable," he said, his voice husky with the cough and the medicine he was taking. "Will you forgive me?"

She found herself weakening. Just as she had done so often in their past encounters. What was it about Edan that had such an effect upon her? She would not let him persuade her this time, though; she would not let him brainwash her. She had come here to help Quinn, if she could, not only to save his job but Rex's life. Once she was sure Edan had come to his senses, she would leave forever.

"I forgive you, certainly. Now, I hope you'll listen to something else I have to say."

Edan closed his eyes as if her attempt to order him about was too much to endure. But Maggie persisted. She had thought about Quinn and his position, and she knew that Edan must be told the facts. He would be very disturbed if Quinn suddenly resigned, without ever giving Edan a chance to help solve the problem.

"When I was in the area one weekend," she began, but he managed to interrupt her before she got any further. His eyes flew open and he turned to look at her in a puzzled way.

"In the area one weekend? Why was that? I don't understand."

"Well, I needed a rest," she said blushing a little. "And I remembered that cottage they rent out at The Bull. You probably haven't even noticed it, but . . ."

"I've noticed it. I'm not blind, you know."

"Sorry. Well, I did rent it just to relax and do some reading. And while I was in the pub having a drink . . ."

"By yourself? That's asking for trouble. You haven't much sense, Miss Jordan. You need someone to tell you what to do, rather than the other way around."

"Please, let me finish. I was having a drink after dinner when Quinn came in with his girlfriend. The one who told my fortune at the camp that night. Do you remember?"

"I remember very well. What has this to do with me?"

"A great deal, I'm afraid. Quinn wants to get married, and the girl, her name is Meta, wants to get married, too. The only way they can do that, with Quinn's prospects, is for him to go back to his people. Quinn wants to stay on here, Edan, he really loves the Park and the horses, and working for you. But he also wants to get married. So I was thinking . . . you have so many farms on the estate, is there a cottage that isn't being used? That Quinn might have?"

Edan stared at her for a long moment, and then said with the first hint of laughter he had shown, "You are a Miss Fix-it, aren't you? How did you come to think of that? Well, never mind, there is a cottage. On one of the farms there's a house and buildings that haven't been used for years. We work the land immediately around them and there hasn't been any need for a tenant. Unfortunately, the house needs repairs. And so do the outbuildings. But I was thinking of working on them. They're very old and they ought to be preserved."

"But that sounds perfect! Would the house be suitable for Quinn if he married?"

"Perfectly. It's a brick cottage with about eight rooms, I think. Space for children and dogs, everything. That might work out very well. You know, Miss Jordan, if you've helped keep Quinn here, you've done me a great service."

"Then you'll talk to Quinn about it right away?"

"Yes, I will."

"And Rex . . . you weren't serious about having Rex put down, were you? I couldn't bear that, Edan, really."

"I never meant it. I was just being bad-tempered. It was because you had disappeared. It made me worry, and I felt neglected. I wouldn't get rid of Rex, you know that."

She felt so relieved to think she hadn't been wrong in her judgment of Edan in that regard. It made her feel good, too, to think she might have helped Quinn with his problems.

"You're not going back to London yet, are you?" Edan asked, waiting for her to pour more tea. "I'm not well, not at all."

"I'll stay, on condition that you eat properly. Everything Mrs. Bateman serves."

When Mrs. Bateman came in to take the tray, Maggie ordered a supper of juice, toast, and scrambled eggs, which she thought would give him quick nourishment. Mrs. Bateman was glad enough to prepare it, and also gratified to see the plate cleaned off, an hour later.

"You're beginning to tire," Maggie said finally. "You really ought to go up to bed, Edan."

"In a minute," he said. "You didn't tell me any news about Brenda. Except that we weren't getting married. Which I already knew. What's happening over at Chagford?"

"Brenda's planning some renovations," she said briefly. "Peter is in charge. That's about all the news."

She wasn't anxious to pursue this line, but Edan immediately became curious.

"Won't that leave you out in the cold? Is the romance all off between you and Peter, then?"

"There was never any romance. He's a good friend, that's all. I told you that before."

"But surely you'll mind him spending all his time with Brenda," Edan went on. "That's quite an assignment."

"His personal life is up to him. I have my own clients and I'm free to deal with them as I see fit."

When he had finished his tea, she ordered him to bed, and he went off somewhat reluctantly, but this time there was no argument.

From then on, Edan ate what he was served and took his pills agreeably. He and Maggie talked about work on the old farm and Quinn was delighted with the news that he would be able to occupy the cottage in the spring. He made plans to marry Meta in April and promised to stay on at Deane Park as long as he was needed.

Each morning Maggie went riding with Quinn.

"You're improving, Miss," he said encouragingly. "One of these days you'll be a fine rider."

"But not as good as Brenda Hawke," she said, with a rueful smile.

"No, Miss," he said truthfully. "You have to be born in the saddle to ride like her. But you'll be fine, just the same."

The days were reaching toward Christmas. Maggie

had planned to spend the holidays with Peter, but now that he was installed at Chagford it didn't seem likely. Once he telephoned, but it was a brief call concerning the office and some billing he had expected her to do for him. She didn't mention Christmas, and neither did he.

Three days before the holiday weekend, she told Edan that she must get back to London.

"I haven't shopped. I haven't made any reservations for dinner, nor have I invited anyone. I'll have to check with Peter," she said, a bit vaguely. "I can't stay here any longer, Edan. I have my career to think of. And my social life."

She felt it was reasonably safe to say these things. Edan was in good spirits and was talking of visiting Farraday and some of the other tenants. Doctor Baker had given him permission to go out if he wrapped up well, but only for short periods of time at first. She could see that he was restless and ready to go back to work. Soon he would be making romantic overtures again, she thought, and life would be just as difficult as before. The sickness had kept him calm, along with the medication that produced lethargy in most patients.

She had brought up the subject of leaving when they were sitting in the rent room after dinner. She had spent time in the past few days fixing it up. One of the carpets from the attic had been cleaned and put down, and she had brought in a few pieces of comfortable furniture from other rooms.

"I'm glad you're allowing me a drink again," Edan said. "I find it relaxing."

"You must eat properly when I'm gone," she said, ignoring his suggestion that she controlled his actions. "Otherwise, you'll just fall sick again."

Edan was sprawled in an armchair before the fire. He had asked Quinn to cut some evergreens and had put them over the mantel. The smell of them was sharp and refreshing. He gave her a long, hard look and held up his glass in a mock toast.

"Merry Christmas! I hope you enjoy yourself in London."

"Thank you. I hope you're happy here."

"I'll be alone," he said.

"You were alone before I ever met you. Surely Brenda will invite you over for dinner during the season? And some of your other friends in the county?"

"I'm not well enough to go bouncing around the countryside in this weather," he said testily. "And I have no hostess. So how can I give dinners here?"

"I'm sorry."

"No, you aren't. You're sure that career comes first?"

"Oh, Edan, nothing's changed. I can't settle for less. And Peter depends on me to keep things running. To carry the load."

"While he's over there having a good time with Brenda? And you think *that's* not chauvinistic? What are you but a donkey?"

"I'm the junior partner. So I expect to carry on when Peter is busy with a client."

Still, now that he had brought it up, it seemed unfair of Peter to expect her to do most of the work while he and Brenda enjoyed themselves at Chagford Hunt. She hadn't thought of it like that before. Yet Peter had not even called to explain his future plans or apologize for putting so much of the load on her. He simply relied on her to do it.

"Very well, Maggie Jordan. If that's what you want."

He was strangely resigned—which was so unlike Edan Deane that she felt out of touch. She had actually steeled herself for a big scene, for shouts, for accusations of abandonment, but he was calm. That was the eerie thing.

"Tell you what," he said, still in a placid voice. "How about a farewell dinner tomorrow night? A pre-holiday party? I could have Mrs. Bateman cook a turkey. And Bateman chill some of my favorite champagne. The Veuve Clicquot-Ponsardin '47 is excellent."

"That would be lovely, Edan."

At bedtime, he said goodnight without any cutting remarks. He made no advances, nor any innuendos. Could Edan Deane have reformed?

On her last day, she rode with Quinn first thing in the morning. She spent the rest of the day roaming about the house. She helped Mrs. Bateman with some Christmas decorations and felt a pang of guilt because she was leaving. Edan was out with the shepherd and did not return for lunch. She felt let down. Yet it was all going smoothly, just as she had hoped. Edan was in good spirits again. Mrs. Bateman could talk to him about the house, about shopping problems, without expecting an explosion of some kind. So Maggie had accomplished her mission. It was time to go.

She felt sad. But she did not allow her feelings to stop her from looking forward to this festive dinner on her final night. She dressed carefully, choosing a long, pale-blue woollen shirtdress, gold chains, and a gold bracelet that Peter had given her for her birthday. She checked her hair, finding it smooth and honey-blonde, and makeup, which was light. It would be flattering in the candlelight that would be part of the dinner arrangements. Her perfume was a new one called Farouche, which had a sweet, rather haunting scent. As she descended the stairs, she was satisfied that she looked her best.

To her amazement, every light in the place was on. And the doors of every room were open: First Drawing Room, library, dining room, and rent room. This was extraordinary, since Edan had been in the habit of ordering them closed.

She found him in the rent room, where they had decided earlier to have their pre-dinner drink, instead of in the library. Edan was pouring himself a whisky and soda.

"And what would you like, Maggie Jordan? This is your special night."

"Whisky and soda, please."

She saw that the painting had been removed. She missed it almost at once.

"What have you done with the painting?"

He knew what she meant without turning around. When he handed her the drink, he said, still without glancing at the wall, "I took it down. It serves no purpose if you aren't here. You're the one who cared whether Lady Caroline painted it."

"I suppose you're right."

Again, she felt his behavior was odd but she could not say why. It was his house and his picture, so of course he could do exactly as he liked.

"I'm not going to make a speech," he said. "I'm not going to beg you to reconsider. So you're wasting your time if you expect it."

"I don't want a speech."

"You could still do the job here. I'd promise to keep out of your way. We could renegotiate the price."

"You said you wouldn't make a speech."

"I'm not. I was only chatting."

"It wouldn't be any use."

"Why wouldn't it? Brenda isn't in the picture anymore, doesn't that count for something? You thought I paid attention to her opinions, you assumed I was going to marry her. But I didn't and I wasn't. Doesn't that count?"

"It isn't only that, Edan," she said carefully. "It's the

whole difference in our outlook. You think that women are second-rate. That you can dictate. That women are little more than servants. Well, I don't agree. I think we're equal, and should be treated in a fair way. *That's* what it's all about."

"I see. You don't think I'm capable of caring enough about any woman to treat her fairly?"

"Why don't we just go in to dinner," she said wearily. "Or all the holiday spirit will evaporate."

Bateman had just removed the soup plates when the telephone rang in the front hall. They had ordered another telephone weeks earlier, but it had not been installed. Bateman came in to say it was for Miss Jordan, and that it was urgent.

"In the middle of dinner?" Edan said, looking annoyed.

"It's Mr. Cross, Milord. He asked particularly that I bring Miss Jordan to the telephone."

"Very well. It's terribly rude of Peter to call in the middle of dinner. Did you tell him we were dining?"

"Yes, Milord."

"I'll take it. Perhaps it's important," Maggie said and laid down her napkin.

At the telephone, she said nervously, "Peter? What on earth's the matter? You know Edan can't bear calls during dinner."

"Merry Christmas, Maggie. I know how Edan feels but I wanted to tell you something I think you ought to know. I mean, it affects you too."

"But what is it? What can possibly be so important?"

"I'm staying on here at Chagford over Christmas," he said.

Maggie felt a swooping, unfamiliar feeling, as if she were suddenly an orphan. Christmas in London, with no escort, no reservations, nothing to do? It was incredible. She had counted on Peter returning to the city for the holidays. He had talked about it long ago.

"But I expected you—I'm driving to the city tomorrow morning. So I'll have time to shop and make some plans. I thought—"

"There's more, Maggie. I have to tell you, my dear, so you can prepare for the future. You see, I'll be staying on here indefinitely. Brenda and I are engaged. We're announcing it Christmas week."

"Engaged?"

She sat down on the chair beside the refectory table. She felt ill.

"Yes, I know it's sudden. But you see, I'm going to restore Chagford completely. It will be the work not of months, but of years. Brenda and I will plan it together—we're going to be married, probably in a month or two. That hasn't been decided yet."

"And the business?" Maggie whispered, still wondering if this was some nightmare that she might wake up from. "Are you letting the business go? What about me?"

"We'll have a meeting about that. After New Year's Day. You'll be all right, my dear. Don't worry. I'll find some work for you in the meantime, and you already have a couple of clients, haven't you? You might consider taking up Edan's offer again."

"I see. Yes. Well, congratulations, Peter."

She hung up, dazed. Then she pulled herself together and went back to the dining room.

"What did he say? You look stunned," Edan observed.

Bateman brought in the fish course.

"It's so strange. . . . I hardly know how to tell you."

"Try," Edan said, while Bateman filled the champagne glasses. "Perhaps a little champers will help."

In fact, he didn't seem as surprised as she had expected.

"Peter's always had his eye on the main chance," Edan said. "And Chagford and Brenda's money are definitely the main chance. His own family lost a great deal of money, as you probably know. So, of course, he realizes what a fortune like Brenda's represents. And certainly he knows what a property like Chagford Hunt represents. It's far more his style than Deane Park, you know."

"I just can't seem to understand."

"Drink up, Maggie Jordan. Fate has dealt you a cruel blow!"

"Oh, stop trying to be funny," she cried, stung by his seeming heartlessness. "You always have to be sarcastic. Can't you see I'm upset?"

"Then perhaps this will be balm to your soul."

He produced from under the table a badly wrapped package. She took it from him with trembling fingers and found it was Lady Caroline's painting. Momentarily, at least, she forgot Peter Cross and his engagement.

"Oh, the painting! But you can't give me this, Edan. It belongs here in Deane Park. It's part of this house! Of the legend."

"It's your going-away present."

"Oh. . . . I can't think of anything to say!"

"You might give me a thank-you kiss," he suggested.

"Yes, yes, I will."

She got up and rushed toward him and kissed him on the cheek. His hand came up to caress her neck. She felt the tide of desire that always welled up when Edan was near, and now it threatened to engulf her. She pulled away hastily.

"Please, don't do that. Not now."

He let her go and she took her place once more.

Bateman brought in the turkey. It was delicious, but Maggie was so upset by the evening's events that she could barely eat. She did manage to drink a fair amount of champagne, however.

Just before Bateman was due to bring in the coffee,

along with a plum pudding and hard sauce especially produced for the evening, there was another interruption. This time it was Quinn.

"But he can't interrupt dinner," Edan protested to Bateman. "He knows perfectly well I won't tolerate it."

But Quinn insisted on coming in. He was reporting that the gelding, which had been ailing earlier in the day, was recovering nicely. He thought the good news would improve his Lordship's evening. Edan groaned.

"I've never had such a dinner!" he complained. "People are taking advantage of me!"

At this moment Rex burst in. But when he saw Maggie, he came up to her and almost pushed her off the chair. She laughed, and at the same time there were tears in her eyes.

"Oh, Rex, dear Rex! I'm going to miss you."

Rex sat staring at her with huge, shining eyes.

"Take that confounded dog out, will you, Quinn? I won't have animals around when I'm eating. This household is falling apart!"

Maggie watched as Rex was taken out. She felt choked. And confused. It was a peculiar evening, where everything went wrong, everything was happening in a way that was impossible. As they waited for the dessert, Bateman burst in with yet another announcement.

"Mrs. Bateman is ill, Milord. I must go to her. I can't serve."

Edan's words at this point were both loud and rude. But Maggie intervened.

"It's all right, Bateman. I'll bring in the coffee and dessert. You go along."

And she hurrried out to the kitchens. As she picked up the tray, she noticed that the door to the butler's pantry was ajar. She could see the edge of Mrs.

Bateman's skirt and hear the murmur of voices. Curious, she set down the tray. There was something going on here that was not aboveboard.

She threw open the pantry door and there, besides the two Batemans, was Quinn.

"Just what is going on?" she said. "Will you please explain to me why everyone is behaving so badly? You aren't sick, Mrs. Bateman! And you, Quinn, you did that deliberately. You deliberately let that dog in. Isn't that right?"

They looked embarrassed. At last Quinn spoke up.

"That's right, Miss."

"But why? Why did you upset Lord Deane like that?"

"It was his orders, Miss," Bateman said quickly. "He ordered all the things that happened. Even Mr. Cross's telephone call."

So it was a trick! Peter's call, the picture as a gift, the dog, and Mrs. Bateman's illness. Just so she would jump in and rescue dinner, showing that she really cared about this house. Well, she would show Edan Deane whether he could play his miserable tricks on her! Cruel! Manipulative! Unutterably selfish!

She burst into the dining room. She spluttered, the words tumbling over one another, she was so furious and so excited.

"How *could* you be so cruel?" she demanded. "Letting me believe Peter was engaged to Brenda just so I wouldn't drive back to London. Then bringing in Rex like that, when you knew it would upset me. And filling me with champagne and pretending to make a gift of the painting. You never intended to let me have that picture, did you? You never meant it to leave this house. Oh, you're despicable!"

Edan came around the table and tried to take her in his arms.

"Now, Maggie, don't go on like that," he said,

realizing that he had upset her far more than he had meant to. "Peter and Brenda really are engaged. I'll admit I asked him to call at this hour to tell you about it. I thought it might make you see there was no future for you in London. Believe me, I only did it to show you how much I want you here, how much I need you to restore Deane Park. I want to be fair."

"Fair? You call that fair? Lying to me? And making up games? Oh, Edan, nothing ever changes with you, does it?"

"I need you. I did it because I was desperate."

Had he really made these plans because he cared so much? He had driven her away in the first place by his difficult behavior, but had he been so lonely that he would do anything, use any device, to win her back?

"I don't believe you."

"Only a man who was wildly in love with a woman would stoop to such tactics!" he cried. "Can't you see that? I can't let you go, Maggie. I'd do all those crazy things and more, if I thought it would keep you here beside me."

"Oh, Edan, you're . . . hopeless."

All the resistance drained out of her. She began to laugh and cry at the same time as he swept her into his arms and held her tighter than he had ever done before. Losing her breath, she tried to beat her fists against him and force him to loosen his hold. But though his grip grew less fierce, she could feel his heart pounding against her own and his mouth was just as demanding as she remembered.

He held her from him and looked down at her, this time with complete love and devotion.

"This may be your last night, Maggie, just as we said when we planned this dinner, but it's not your last night at Deane Park—and he picked her up and carried her out of the room, across the front hall and up the stairs. "It's your last night as Maggie Jordan, because after

tomorrow you're going to be mine—you're going to be
Maggie Deane. I'll get special permission to marry you
tomorrow."

"You can't do that," she said. "There are laws."

But his words filled her with intoxicating sweetness
and a flood of desire drowned all reason.

"You'll see, a lord can perform magic," he said at the
top of the stairs. "Otherwise what's the use of having
privileges? A lord can command a special dispensation.
I'll arrange it—don't worry."

"Edan, we can't get married tomorrow. It's impossible. But I love you for trying."

"Do you love me, Maggie?" he said and hesitated.
"Do you love me enough to give up your career and
stay here with me forever? Because that's what I'm
asking. Do you see how I've reformed? I'm not telling,
I'm asking."

"I heard," she whispered. "I really do think you've
changed. And I'll have to give up my career because it
will take me the rest of my life to restore Deane Park."

He set her down long enough to open the door to his
bedroom. Then he said, with just a glint of his old
humor, "That's what I like to hear, Maggie, my angel.
A woman who knows her place."

She was instantly furious.

"Oh, you haven't changed a bit!"

She tried to flee but he caught her hand and she could
not shake loose. Then he picked her up once more and
took her into the darkened room.

She knew it was useless to fight him any longer. She
felt like a swimmer in a dreamlike lake, floating on
beautiful clear water, floating toward some blissful
shore. There was no more resistance left in her. No
more anger or fear of loneliness. She surrendered now
to the need she had secretly harbored ever since the day
when they had met by the stream and he had kissed
her. That was the first time in her life she had known

what ecstasy was. She felt it again now. And nothing else mattered. Only Edan and Edan's kisses.

He put her gently upon the bed. And from his great height, he looked down upon her beauty with overwhelming love.

"Remember, my darling, this is your last night as Maggie Jordan, career girl. Tomorrow, you'll be Lady Deane."

She gazed back at him and knew this was what she had hoped for, what she had wanted since the first moment she had seen Deane Park. As if he could read her thoughts, Edan said softly, "'Lady Moon, Lady Moon, where are you roving?'"

"'Over the sea,'" Maggie whispered.

"'Lady Moon, Lady Moon, whom are you loving?'"

"You who love me," she said, altering the words to make it a final, loving pact. She was certain Houghton, the poet, wouldn't mind.

She knew then that this was paradise. As Edan's lips came down on hers, and she felt his body warm and loving against her own, she thought for just a tiny moment in time that she heard the faint trill of a woman's laughter. Far away. But perhaps it was just the call of some bird that felt the happiness which had fallen upon Deane Park at last.

Silhouette Romance

IT'S YOUR OWN SPECIAL TIME

*Contemporary romances for today's women.
Each month, six very special love stories will be yours
from SILHOUETTE. Look for them wherever books are sold
or order now from the coupon below.*

$1.50 each

Hampson	☐ 1 ☐ 4 ☐ 16 ☐ 27 ☐ 28 ☐ 52 ☐ 94	Browning	☐ 12 ☐ 38 ☐ 53 ☐ 73 ☐ 93
Stanford	☐ 6 ☐ 25 ☐ 35 ☐ 46 ☐ 58 ☐ 88	Michaels	☐ 15 ☐ 32 ☐ 61 ☐ 87
		John	☐ 17 ☐ 34 ☐ 57 ☐ 85
Hastings	☐ 13 ☐ 26	Beckman	☐ 8 ☐ 37 ☐ 54 ☐ 96
Vitek	☐ 33 ☐ 47 ☐ 84	Wisdom	☐ 49 ☐ 95
Wildman	☐ 29 ☐ 48	Halston	☐ 62 ☐ 83

☐ 5 Goforth	☐ 22 Stephens	☐ 50 Scott	☐ 81 Roberts
☐ 7 Lewis	☐ 23 Edwards	☐ 55 Ladame	☐ 82 Dailey
☐ 9 Wilson	☐ 24 Healy	☐ 56 Trent	☐ 86 Adams
☐ 10 Caine	☐ 30 Dixon	☐ 59 Vernon	☐ 89 James
☐ 11 Vernon	☐ 31 Halldorson	☐ 60 Hill	☐ 90 Major
☐ 14 Oliver	☐ 36 McKay	☐ 63 Brent	☐ 92 McKay
☐ 19 Thornton	☐ 39 Sinclair	☐ 71 Ripy	☐ 97 Clay
☐ 20 Fulford	☐ 43 Robb	☐ 76 Hardy	☐ 98 St. George
☐ 21 Richards	☐ 45 Carroll	☐ 78 Oliver	☐ 99 Camp

$1.75 each

Stanford	☐ 100 ☐ 112 ☐ 131	Hampson	☐ 108 ☐ 119 ☐ 128 ☐ 136 ☐ 147 ☐ 151 ☐ 155
Hardy	☐ 101 ☐ 130		
Cork	☐ 103 ☐ 148	Browning	☐ 113 ☐ 142
Vitek	☐ 104 ☐ 139 ☐ 157	Michaels	☐ 114 ☐ 146
Dailey	☐ 106 ☐ 118 ☐ 153	Beckman	☐ 124 ☐ 154
Bright	☐ 107 ☐ 125	Roberts	☐ 127 ☐ 143

Silhouette Desire
15-Day Trial Offer

A new romance series that explores contemporary relationships in exciting detail

Four Silhouette Desire romances, free for 15 days!
We'll send you four new Silhouette Desire romances to look over for 15 days, absolutely free! If you decide not to keep the books, return them and owe nothing.

Four books a month, free home delivery. If you like Silhouette Desire romances as much as we think you will, keep them and return your payment with the invoice. Then we will send you four new books every month to preview, just as soon as they are published. You pay only for the books you decide to keep, and you never pay postage and handling.

Silhouette Romance

Coming next month from
Silhouette Romances

Logic Of The Heart by Dixie Browning

Emma was looking forward to seeing the romantic island of Hatteras, and meeting Dan Slater added to the magic. She could see herself slipping into his arms and falling under his spell. . . .

Devil's Bargain by Elaine Camp

Was Alexis being caught up in an evil scheme or was Drayce's renewed love for her genuine? Their once passionate marriage seemed too distant to recapture those lost moments of ecstasy. Yet suddenly Drayce made Alexis forget why escape was so important!

Flight To Romance by Tracy Sinclair

Jennifer was not going to refuse Kalim Al Kahira, when he asked her to return with him to Egypt. She told herself her career demanded that she go—until she realized that there was no way to refuse his dark, penetrating eyes.

In Name Only by Roxanne Jarrett

Jill traveled to Brazil to enter into an arranged marriage. She was determined not to be ruled by her new husband, but soon she found herself unable to deny the mad passions that filled her with desire.

Sweet Surrender by Donna Vitek

Suzanne's trip to Italy turned out to be anything but the quiet visit she anticipated. For once she met Jared Caine she felt compelled to compete for his attention and show him the depth and breadth of her love.

The Second Time by Janet Dailey

Dawn returned home to the Florida Keys to seek peace in the turquoise waters. But soon calm waters are turned into turbulent seas when passions are ignited by her old flame Slater MacBride.